JESSICA BECK

CAST IRON MOTIVE

THE FOURTH CAST IRON COOKING MYSTERY

To P & E,
My reasons why!

When the twins' estranged Aunt Della's life is threatened by an unknown assailant, Annie and Pat must leave their beloved Iron and travel deep into the North Carolina mountains to figure out who's trying to kill her before it's too late.

CHAPTER 1: PAT

"**I**S THAT YOU, PATRICK?" AN oddly familiar voice asked me after I answered the phone at the Cast Iron Store and Grill, the combination general store/diner/post office that my fraternal twin sister, Annie, and I owned and operated together. I handled the main shopping area in front, Annie took care of the grill, Edith Bost oversaw the post office, and Skip Lawson was just about everybody else's assistant. Between the four of us, we found a way to make it all work and still manage to turn a modest profit every month.

"It is," I said. "How may I help you?"

"This is Della."

"*Aunt* Della?" I asked. My mother's sister hadn't been in contact with any of us for a great many years, so why was she calling me now? Della had instigated a massive fight with Mom over her marriage to my father on her wedding day, and according to family lore, as the years passed by, the rift continued to build until, at my sixth birthday party—Annie's too, of course—it had all come to a head, and Della had stormed off once and for all. The woman hadn't even had the decency to come to the joint funerals we'd held for our parents two decades later. As far as I knew, it was the last time any of us had heard from her.

As far as I knew.

"Yes, it's your aunt. How have you been, Patrick?" she asked timidly.

"Actually, I go by Pat these days, and I'm just dandy. Thanks for asking," I said. "Listen, I'm kind of busy right now."

"Please don't hang up," she pled.

"I suppose I can spare a minute. Is there something I can do for you?"

"Pat, someone's trying to kill me, and I don't know where else to turn. Won't you please help me?"

———◆◇◆———

"What makes you think *I* can help?" I asked her after taking a moment to catch my breath.

"Just because I haven't been in touch with you directly doesn't mean that I haven't been keeping tabs on all three of you," she said. "I know you and your twin sister have become quite adept at solving murder, and now I need you to save my life."

"You should really call Kathleen," I said. The news that Della had been aware of me and my siblings without us realizing it all those years disturbed me a little, but I'd deal with that later.

"Actually, she's the one who suggested that I contact you," Della said hesitantly.

"You've spoken with *Kathleen*?" I asked icily. My older sister—who also happened to be the sheriff of Maple Crest, North Carolina—was probably the logical choice for her to contact first, but it still stung a little that our long-lost aunt had reached out to her before she'd given Annie or me a call.

"We've been in touch for a few years now," she admitted. "I may live in Gateway Lake, but that doesn't mean that I'm completely isolated from the rest of the world."

"I'm having trouble wrapping my mind around this, Della. You're telling me that you've been in touch with Kathleen for years, and my older sister didn't think it was worth mentioning?" Was there any chance that could be true? "I just don't believe it."

"Don't blame your older sister for not telling you. I didn't want you to know, and I made her promise not to breathe a word of our reconnection to you."

"Does Annie know?" I could find a way to accept behavior from Kathleen that I would never tolerate from Annie. Sharing a womb together, though not the same egg, worked that way, at least as far as I was concerned. If Annie had kept this from me, there was going to be serious trouble between us.

"Of course not," she said. "I wouldn't dream of having her deceive you."

"But it was okay to ask Kathleen to," I said a little petulantly. This woman, my aunt, seemed to have a way of bringing out the worst side of me.

"I never meant to hurt you," she said haltingly.

Well, it was a little too late for that now. Larry Wilson, a retired schoolteacher and frequent customer at the Iron, approached the register with an old-fashioned straw broom made with a twisted wood handle. "Listen, I can't talk right now," I said. "Can I call you back later?"

"Certainly," Della said, and then she recited her number, which I wrote on a brown paper bag. "Please hurry, though. I don't know how much time I have before the next attempt."

Was my aunt being overly dramatic, or did she honestly believe that her death was imminent? I had no way of knowing, since my recollections of the woman were shadowy at best. I could remember her taking us to Rock Lake to swim in the quarry, and the picnic feasts we'd have afterwards, but that was about the sum total of my memories, besides a sporadic Christmas or birthday recollection here and there.

"Troubles, Pat?" Larry asked me.

"No, why do you ask?" I asked as I rang up his purchase.

"You look as though someone just punched you in the gut," he said. "That's a pretty callous expression, isn't it?"

"I've heard worse," I said. Trying to put on a smile I didn't feel, I said, "I'd offer to bag that for you, but I don't have one that's big enough to hold it."

"It's a gag gift for my bride," he said happily. He and his "bride" had been married forever, but their love appeared to be just as fresh as the day it had first been minted. I envied him that, but I was in a new relationship that had promise, so it might just turn out to be "happily ever after" for me as well, though it was much too soon to tell yet.

"Are you sure it's a good idea to give your wife a broom?" I asked him with a smile.

"No worries, it's an inside joke," he said as he took his change. "Patrick, is there anything I can do to help?" he asked softly.

"Thanks, but I've got it under control." The truth was anything but that, but I wasn't about to share my problems with the retired schoolteacher. That was one of the nice things about living in a small town, though. Help was usually around the corner, and all it took was a simple request for assistance to get more than enough volunteers.

I didn't even know where to begin, though.

After Larry was gone, I walked quickly back to the grill, where Annie was busily preparing lunch for three of our customers. She saw me and raised an eyebrow, asking in our silent language what was going on. I shrugged as I frowned to indicate that we had a situation on our hands, and she raised both eyebrows in response, asking if I needed her instantly.

I shook my head and then glanced to the front. It said to her that when she got the first chance, she needed to come see me, but I didn't want to deprive her customers of their orders. The situation might have been urgent in Della's mind, but that didn't mean that it was imperative for me to act quickly.

Besides, I had a phone call to make before I took this any further.

"Kathleen, how could you?"

My older sister hesitated before answering the question. "Do you want to calm down, Pat? How could I what?" she asked.

"Talk to our aunt for years without telling me," I said fiercely. "I can't believe you'd lie to me."

"When exactly did I lie to you, little brother?" she asked me defiantly.

"Omission is just as big a lie as commission, and you know it," I said.

I could hear Kathleen let out a heavy sigh before she replied. "You're right. I shouldn't have kept it from you. It was wrong to do it, and I'm sorry."

It was a rare apology from her, but I wasn't about to take the time to savor it. "Did you tell Annie about it?"

"No, of course not. Della made me swear that I wouldn't breathe a word about it to either one of you," Kathleen said. "Besides, what are the odds that she'd be able to keep a secret from you?"

"Since when have I been so fragile that I need to be protected from what's going on?" I asked her, raising my voice and not caring who overheard me.

"Well, not to put too fine a point on it, but your reaction right now is a prime example," she said.

"That's garbage, and you know it, Kathleen," I said. "If you two are so close, why didn't *you* volunteer to help her? Why drag Annie and me into it?"

"I would if I could, but there's no way I can leave town right now," she said. "Hank is on vacation for the next two weeks, and I can't leave the department in Ginny's hands. She's too young, and she hasn't been at this long enough to know how to handle things. When Della first told me about what was going on, I offered to help her, but when I told her that it was going to be a few weeks before I could get there, she said that she wasn't at all sure that she'd still be alive then."

"Is there any chance she's just being overdramatic?" I asked. I remembered our aunt as being flamboyant, a little larger than life.

"Not this time. You don't know her as well as I do," Kathleen said.

"Is it *my* fault that she didn't reach out to me?" I asked angrily.

"Pat, take a deep breath and at least hear me out. This isn't like you, and you know it."

"Kathleen, she didn't even come to Mom and Dad's funerals," I said, fighting back angry tears.

"Della was out of the country when the car wreck happened," Kathleen explained. "She felt terrible about missing her last chance to say good-bye."

"I wish I could find a little sympathy for her, but I just can't, not given the fact that the rift was her fault to begin with," I replied.

"Be that as it may, whether you like it or not, she's the closest thing to family that the three of us have left. When family needs you, you answer the call."

"Even given these particular circumstances?" I asked her.

"Especially because of them. What if she's right, and she's murdered before you and Annie have a chance to help her? How are you going to feel having that on your conscience, that you might have been able to save her?"

Leave it to my big sister to use the voice of reason with me. I'd had a tough time going against her will when we'd been kids, and it still didn't come all that easily to me. "Let me talk to Annie," I said in exasperation as I saw my fraternal twin approach the front.

"Good. I'll be right over," Kathleen said, the relief clear in her voice.

Before she could hang up, I said, "Do me a favor and don't."

Kathleen was clearly hurt as she replied, "Seriously, Pat? Are you really going to hold this against me?"

"Just let Annie and me talk first," I said.

After a moment of hesitation, she asked, "Will you at least call me and tell me what you decide to do? I might be able to get an old friend from April Springs to come up and babysit the department for me if I need to go."

"Do you trust her with that?" I asked, surprised that my sister would let anyone run her department for her.

"It happens to be a 'he,' and he used to be a state police inspector before he retired to marry a donutmaker," she said. "He's one of the best cops I've ever known, but I'd hate to call him unless it's an emergency. I heard that he just quit as acting police chief in the small town where they live, and I've got the feeling that he's taking a well-earned break from law enforcement."

"We'll let you know the second we decide what we're going to do," I said, and then I hung up and faced Annie. "We need to talk."

"No lie. I could hear you shouting at someone on the phone from the grill. Who were you talking to just now?"

"Kathleen," I said.

"Our big sister, Kathleen?" Annie asked, her eyes going wide. "Do you have a death wish, little brother?"

Annie was every bit of seven minutes older than I was, but she loved reminding me every chance she got. "Aunt Della called me a few minutes ago. She asked me for our help."

The smile suddenly vanished from Annie's face. "Tell me everything."

———————

After I brought my twin sister up to date, she frowned for a moment before answering. "We have to help her if we can. You know that, don't you?"

"Annie, we can't leave the store any more than Kathleen can shut down the police force," I said in protest. Why was my twin sister so favorable to the idea of going to our aunt's aid, when the woman had done nothing to be a part of our lives for decades?

"Nonsense. We can at least give her three or four days," Annie said. "Skip can run the front, and I can get Lindsey to take over the grill while we're gone."

"You'd seriously let her handle things in your domain?" I asked. Lindsey was more a friend of my sister's than of mine, and I knew that she'd taken to cast iron cooking, but I had no idea that Annie held her talents in that high esteem.

"Why not? She's been taking classes from me for years," Annie reminded me. "You know as well as I do that I've even had her sub for me here before."

"For an hour or two at a time, at most," I said. "Three or four days is an entirely different beast."

"She can handle it," Annie said. "We have to do this, Patrick."

Why did people keep insisting on calling me by my complete first name? It rarely meant anything good for me. Given Annie's tone, I knew that there was no way I could fight this. It was happening, whether I liked it or not. "Fine. I'll call her and let her know that we'll be there this evening," I said as I reached for the paper bag that had Della's phone number written on it.

"Do you mind if I call her myself?" Annie asked me tentatively.

"Are you sure you want to?"

"Pat, I'm the only one in the family that she *hasn't* contacted. Sure, I'd like to talk to her. I have so many fond memories of her and Mom together. They were always making each other laugh, remember?"

"Sure, unless they were talking about Dad," I said, still holding onto that particular grudge.

Matter-of-factly, Annie said, "She was wrong about him, as we both well know, but that's no reason not to help her."

I reluctantly handed my twin the number. "Here you go. After you're finished, call Kathleen and tell her that we're planning to go."

"Pat, are you really okay with us doing this?" she asked me.

"Do I honestly have a choice?" I asked with the hint of a grin.

"Not really," she replied with a smile of her own. "You should tell Skip what we're planning, and I'll phone Lindsey. After we close the store for the day, we can head out. If we leave by five, we should be able to get there by seven tonight."

"Wow, you're really serious about making this happen right away, aren't you?"

"Like I said, what choice do we have?"

"Okay, you both win," I said. "I was never any good at holding out when you and Kathleen ganged up on me."

Annie took my hands in hers. "Pat, we don't have to do this if you're that much against it."

"I may not be all that happy about it, but I know in my heart that you're both right. It's what family does."

"Maybe not all of them, but we do," she said.

As Annie dialed our aunt's phone number to tell her that we'd be on our way later that evening, I called Skip up front to tell him the news.

"To be honest with you, it's not a great time for me," Skip said reluctantly after I told him that he'd be in charge of the store for the next four days. I'd been expecting a little more enthusiasm on his part.

"Why not? Do you have other plans?"

"Not exactly. I was just about ready to ask you for a few days off myself. I've been working on a new glaze in my pottery studio that I think is going to be a real winner this time." Skip was constantly trying to come up with new ways to make money, often by making crafty objects that he tried selling in our shop. I'd given him a shelf in the store, but so far, he hadn't found a way to turn much of a profit on it.

"I'm afraid that it's going to have to wait until we get back," I said.

"Fine. Sure. I'd be happy to do it. Does that mean that I get a bump in pay?" he asked me with a grin, which told me that he was going to be fine with the idea.

I mentioned a sum, and his eyes brightened. "Per hour?"

"No, that's the total amount for the entire time we're gone." The lights in his gaze dimmed a little, so maybe I should sweeten the pot a little. "How about if we give you an extra shelf to sell more of your wares as well? It might give you a little more incentive to work hard."

"Two shelves isn't that much better than one. Do you have anything else you can offer?"

"How about keeping your job? Isn't that incentive enough?" I asked him with a smile.

"Four shelves," he countered.

"Two," I said, holding fast to my original offer.

"Can you at least go to three?"

I had to laugh. "Fine. But I get to pick the shelves," I said. We walked through the store, and I found enough items we could consolidate to make more room for him to expand his footprint. "This is temporary, remember?"

"What if my offerings outsell what's already there?" he asked.

"We'll increase your space if you do well enough, but you'd better not start hard-selling our clientele, or you'll lose what you've got."

"Are you kidding? I wouldn't dream of doing that," he said.

"Because our customers would complain about it as soon as we got back to the Iron?" I asked him with a laugh.

"They wouldn't even wait that long. They'd call you while you were still out of town," he agreed. "No strong-arm tactics. It will be a fair test. You can trust me."

I put an arm around him. "Don't you think I know that? After all, I'm trusting you with something I love dearly. I know you won't let me down."

"You bet I won't," my young employee answered. "You can count on me."

At least that was taken care of.

As the workday came to a close, I was surprised to see Kathleen come into the Iron.

I had to guess that Annie had already updated her on our plans.

So why was she there?

"Hey," I said noncommittally as I finished cashing out the register. I still needed to pack for the trip, and we had a long drive ahead of us, so I wasn't in the mood for small talk, especially with my older sister.

Kathleen reached into her pocket and pulled out a white kerchief, which she proceeded to wave in the air in front of my face. "How about a truce? I come in peace."

It was hard to resist, but I was still angry with her for holding out on us about Della. "I'm sorry, but I can't just forgive and forget that easily."

"I understand," she said. I hated it when she was reasonable with me. It made arguing with her that much harder. "Take your time. How about now?" she asked after a brief pause.

"Kathleen, if you tell me you did it for my own good, I'm going to scream," I said.

"I wouldn't think of it. This was all about Aunt Della's wants and needs. The truth is she was afraid to face you and Annie."

"Why would she be scared of us? You're the most terrifying one of the three of us, by far."

My older sister grinned. "As much as I appreciate the compliment, it's not entirely true. I may be able to face down criminals, but when it comes to family issues, you and Annie are much scarier than I could ever be."

"Kathleen, do you honestly believe her? Is her life really in jeopardy?" I asked, deciding that I was projecting my anger at the wrong family member.

"She sounded pretty convincing to me," my older sister said. "You two need to watch your backs while you're up there, okay? In Maple Crest, you know just about all of the players, but you'll be on strange turf up there, and danger could come from a direction that you least expect."

"You sound as though you're having second thoughts about sending Aunt Della to us."

Kathleen frowned. "I called my friend after we spoke, but he and his wife were on their way out of town. It appears that they have family problems of their own they need to deal with."

"Sounds like there's a lot of that going around," I said. "Any idea as to how we approach this thing with Aunt Della?"

"Try to get as many hard facts as you can, and go from there. I don't have to tell you two how to snoop around. You've become pretty proficient at it. Just be careful, okay?"

Her compliment was unexpected, and it was evident that she was concerned about us. To her surprise, I leaned forward and hugged her. "Thanks for caring so much."

"I try," she said, holding onto me a split second longer than I'd expected. When we broke our hug, I could see that she was smiling. "Have you told your girlfriend that you're leaving town suddenly?" she asked me.

"I don't know if we're at that stage yet," I said.

"What, keeping her informed of your whereabouts?"

"No, officially calling her my girlfriend. To answer your question, Jenna knows that we're going," I said. As a matter of fact, I'd called her at the same time Annie had been phoning Della.

"What did she say to that?"

"She just told me to be careful," I said.

"How about Annie? Has she made that call herself?"

I grinned at Kathleen. "Why would Annie call Jenna?"

"I'm talking about Timothy, and you know it."

"I don't know. You'll have to ask her. Now, if you'll excuse me, I've got to close up for the day, pack a bag, and hit the road."

"Call me if you need me," Kathleen said as she took the hint and headed for the door.

"You bet," I said.

"On second thought, let me know when you get there."

I saluted. "Will do, but we'll never be able to leave if you keep hanging around here," I said with a grin. "Don't you want to say good-bye to Annie?"

Kathleen shook her head. "There's no need. We already had a nice long chat on the phone."

I glanced back to see my twin grinning at both of us. There was no doubt in my mind that she'd urged Kathleen to come by so we could patch things up before we left, and I would have resented her meddling if I hadn't been so happy that she'd done it. I hated being at odds with either of my siblings.

At least now I could leave town with a clear conscience.

CHAPTER 2: ANNIE

"**A**RE YOU RESPONSIBLE FOR WHAT just happened?" my brother, Pat, asked me as he walked back to the grill. I was cleaning up my cast iron pots and skillets that I'd used that day, giving them light coats of oil and then putting them into the ovens at low heat to help the metal absorb more of the oil that kept the seasoning intact. It had become a ritual as ingrained in me as brushing my teeth every morning after breakfast. I knew that if I took care of my ironware, it would last long after I was gone.

"What are you talking about?" I asked, feigning ignorance. Why did he even have to ask? Of course I'd told Kathleen that she had to come over after hearing about Pat's reaction to Della's news. My brother could be pigheaded at times, which proved that we weren't twins in *every* way, no matter what anybody else might say about my own stubborn streak.

"Annie, the truth."

"Of course I told her to come by, Pat. You can't hold it against Kathleen. It wasn't her fault."

My brother looked at me skeptically. "Do you mean to tell me that you're not upset?"

"Absolutely," I said. "I hate the idea that someone may actually be trying to kill our aunt."

"I'm talking about Kathleen being in contact with Aunt Della all of this time without telling either one of us about it," Pat said as he sat at the bar where I normally served my customers.

"I'm sure she had her reasons," I said. In all honesty, I'd been a little miffed when I'd first heard about it, but those feelings had quickly been overcome by what Aunt Della had told me about her situation. She hadn't gone into great detail, but it was clear that she was afraid for her life. If Pat and I could help her, I didn't see any way that we could decline the request.

"I don't know. Maybe you're right. I just seem to be having trouble getting past everything," Pat said. "Have you told Timothy what we're doing yet?"

"I gave him the news, but I'm not exactly sure that he heard me," I said with a smile.

"Is he being distracted by his construction project? How's the cabin coming along?" Pat asked me. My boyfriend, Timothy, had bought land next to mine, and with the proceeds from a windfall too detailed to get into, he'd used the money to put up a cabin of his own. It had become an obsession with him, and with me as well, since I also chose to live in a cabin in the woods. My brother preferred living in town, though how he handled living in an apartment above the store was beyond me. I needed space around me, room to breathe, and a chance to get away from being constantly reminded of work, but to each her own. It seemed to work for him, but it would have driven me mad.

"It's right on course," I said. "He's hoping to start stacking logs this week."

"Wow, that's real progress," Pat said. "Are you okay with missing that?"

"It's not ideal," I confessed, "but what choice do we have?"

"I just hope this isn't some wild-goose chase," Pat said.

"Do you think that's possible?" I asked.

"Annie, what are the odds that someone is really trying to kill our aunt? What could the motivation possibly be?"

"I don't know, but she sounded pretty convincing to me on the phone."

"I know," Pat said with a sigh. "I'll have the deposit ready in ten minutes. How long will you need before we get out of here?"

"I'm just about finished. Don't worry about directions to her place. She gave me pretty detailed instructions," I said as I reached over and turned the ovens off. The pots, skillets, and lids would all cool there overnight and be ready for use the next day. I jotted a quick note to Lindsey to that effect, since I'd already called her three times with further instructions. What it boiled down to was that I either trusted her, or I didn't. It was just harder than I'd thought it would be leaving my precious grill to someone else, even if it was only for four days max.

"Okay. Should we take your car or my truck?" Pat asked me.

"Why don't you follow me out to my place, and we can leave your truck there until we get back?" I suggested.

"That sounds like a lot of trouble to me. You could always go home and pack a bag, then drive back here and pick me up. I need to finish up a few things around here and then run out and make the deposit. Go grab some stuff and meet me back here."

"Coward," I said with a grin. "You just don't want to tackle my driveway."

"I'm not denying it," he said with a grin of his own. "That road is treacherous."

"It's cute that you think it's a road," I said. "I prefer to think of it more as a beaten path."

"And not a very beaten one at that," he said. "On second thought, would you mind dropping off the deposit for me? It's on your way."

"No worries, little brother. I'll handle it," I said.

Five minutes later, I'd stopped off at the bank and was on my way home to pack enough clothes for four days. It would be strange seeing Aunt Della again. I wasn't even sure that I'd be able to recognize her. After all, Pat and I had been small children the last time she'd been in our lives. We had a lot of catching up to do, but this wasn't just some kind of awkward family reunion.

We were going with a purpose in mind, and that was to see if someone was actually trying to kill our estranged aunt.

"Howdy, stranger. Climb on in," I said as I pulled my Subaru up in front of the Iron to pick Pat up. "Going far?"

"Tell me you don't usually pick up hitchhikers," my brother said as he leaned in through the open passenger's-side window.

"Not as a general rule, but you look harmless enough," I said as he opened the back and threw his bag in the back seat. As we headed north toward Gateway Lake, I asked him, "Do you have any ideas about how we should tackle this situation?"

"Not really. Don't forget, I've had just as much notice about this mess as you have," he said a little grumpily.

I wasn't about to put up with that for the next two hours. I waited until his attention was distracted by his cellphone at the same time that the road was clear, and I jerked the Subaru's steering wheel so that we would be directly in oncoming traffic, if there had been any. I returned the wheel to its proper place just as abruptly, and Pat involuntarily yelped out a little. "Annie, what just happened?"

"Squirrel," I said, doing my best to keep a straight face.

"Well, next time, give me some warning," he said as he looked back over his shoulder for the nonexistent bushy-tailed rodent.

"Hey, he didn't let me know that he was going to dart in front of me at the last second, so how could I tell you?"

"Was there even a squirrel back there?"

"Who's to say it isn't true, just because you might not have seen him," I said. "Now that I have your attention though, I want to say something. Are you listening, or do I have to suddenly dodge something again to get it?"

"I knew there wasn't any squirrel in the road," he said.

"Pat, you have my blessing to fuss and fume for the next ninety-seven seconds, but after that, I expect you to get over your fit of pique once and for all. Your time starts," I paused to wait for the clock on my dash to change over to the next minute before I continued, "now."

"That's not fair. You have no way of knowing precisely when my time is up," he said with a grin.

"Is that really how you want to use your free complaint time?" I asked him, smiling back.

"I don't need it," he said after sighing deeply. "I'm sorry. You're right. I'll do my best, but I can't make any promises. I can't seem to let this go." I was about to crow over his confession that I'd been right, and he knew it, so he quickly added, "It was bound to happen sooner or later, so don't gloat about it."

"I wouldn't dream of doing that," I said, trying my best not to laugh out loud. "Now that we've settled that once and for all…" I paused as I glanced over in his direction. "We *have* settled it for good, right?"

"I said that I'd try," he said. "I don't know what else I can say."

"That's all that I can ask, that you make an effort. We need a strategy."

"I've been thinking about that," Pat said, "and I believe we have to treat this as though it's a case that doesn't involve someone we're so closely related to. First, we need to establish if Della is lying to us, if she's simply mistaken, or if she's correct in believing that someone is trying to kill her."

"Why did you put the idea up that she might be telling the truth last?" I asked him. "Is there some significance to the order?"

"Now you're just sounding paranoid."

"Hey, sometimes paranoid people are right. Sometimes there really is someone out to get them."

"I promise you that I'm going to keep an open mind, but just because she's family doesn't mean that we have to take her word for everything."

"You sound like Ronald Reagan. Trust but verify, right?"

"That was a little before our time, wasn't it?" Pat asked me.

"Sure, but I can read. Can't you?"

He grimaced a little. "This is turning out to be a fun field trip, isn't it?" he commented sarcastically.

"It has potential," I said. I was glad that Pat was going to try to get back to his old self. I just hoped he could manage it once we met or, more appropriately, caught up with Aunt Della again. I loved my brother more than life itself, but he could drive me batty sometimes. I was sure that he could say the same thing about me, and who knows? We were probably both right. He might have been reluctant to get involved with our estranged aunt again, but I had to fight the temptation to drive to Gateway Lake even faster than the speed limit allowed. There was a great deal I'd missed by not having her in my life, and I for one was eager to make up for lost time. That was why it was so imperative for us to make sure that she was safe. I knew that Pat would do his best as well to solve the case, at any rate. After all, deep down, he was a good guy. How could he not be? We were fraternal twins, which wasn't quite identical, but it was still a bond deeper than many siblings shared. "What do we do, start grilling her as soon as we arrive?"

"I'll allow a little time for us all to get reacquainted," he said magnanimously.

"How long?"

"Ninety-seven seconds sounds about right to me," he replied with a smile.

"It's going to take considerably longer than that."

"That's fine, but just remember, every minute we're not trying to get to the truth is potentially another minute that her life is in danger."

"When you put it that way, I have a hard time disagreeing."

"Don't you just love when that happens?" he asked as his smile reappeared.

"Not so much, but I'll let that one slide. So, we say our hellos, then we dig straight into her suspicions and see where they lead us. It's not much of a plan, as far as plans go, is it?"

Pat just shrugged. "I know it's not perfect. That's why I'm open to suggestions."

"I just wish I had one," I said.

The rest of the drive went much better, and after passing the town limit sign for Gateway Lake, I felt the butterflies in my stomach doing belly flops. I was about to connect with my mother's sister, a link that I'd nearly lost forever. There were banners draped across the main road proclaiming something called the Winter Wonderland, and I could see different decorations still up from what must have been a fairly recent event. Plastic snowflakes hung down from the light posts, and eight-foot-tall wooden snowmen were placed everywhere. Most of them had been painted the traditional white, but some sported colors as different as psychedelic tie-dye all the way to flannel patterns to ones draped with old Christmas lights. It appeared that we'd just missed the festivities, but that was fine with me.

My hands began to tighten on the steering wheel. I was surprised to find that I was nervous about the coming encounter. I glanced over at my brother, who was chewing his bottom lip. "Are you anxious about seeing her again?"

"Not particularly," Pat said absently, and then he must have realized how callous it must have sounded. "I didn't mean that in a bad way. It's just that we've got a pretty daunting task in front of us. Back in Maple Crest, we know just about everybody in town. We're strangers here, and no one has any reason to answer our questions, let alone trust us."

"Don't you think the fact that we're Aunt Della's family will count for something?"

"Maybe, maybe not," he said. "Then again, if someone's trying to kill her and she can't even figure out who it is, it may mean that she's made herself some enemies here."

I patted his leg. "Don't worry, Pat. There's two of us and only one person trying to kill her. Whoever wants her dead doesn't stand a chance."

"I hope you're right. How much farther is it?"

"Based on the instructions Aunt Della gave me, it should just be a few minutes now," I said.

CHAPTER 3: PAT

"REMEMBER TO SMILE," ANNIE TOLD me as she pulled up in front of a dated cottage in bad need of a fresh coat of paint. A streetlight in front of the place illuminated it brighter than it should have been for that time of evening during winter, at least as far as I was concerned. There was an old Volkswagen Beetle parked in the driveway, but I wasn't even sure it still ran based on its outward appearance. I could see several weeds poking out of the flower beds in front, the annuals that had been killed by the first frost serving as dreary reminders that spring was still a lifetime away.

"She's not even out here waiting for us," I said. "She does know we're coming, right?"

"What do you want, a sign and a handful of balloons?" Annie asked me brightly.

"Fine. Let's go knock on the front door."

"Should we grab our bags first?" Annie asked me.

"Why don't we wait and see how it goes?" I suggested.

"Pat, we're staying here with her. I've already worked that out."

"Are you sure she has the room?" I asked, looking around the small space. "She wants us to stay with her, right?"

"Why wouldn't she? After all, we're both quite charming. I happen to come by it naturally, but with you it takes a little effort."

"But worth it all the same, right?" I asked her. My sister's good humor was infectious. If she didn't hold a grudge over what had happened so long ago, then how could I? I resolved to stop paying lip service to my promise to behave and actually try to mean it. I'd had a friend once who believed in faking it until you made it, and he'd managed to get ahead with an extraordinarily short supply of talent, but it had taken a great deal of audacity to overcome its absence.

"Let's go say hi," Annie said, and I followed her to the door.

When we got there, my sister didn't knock at first.

"Any time is fine with me," I said after a few moments of delay.

"Aren't you the least bit curious about what we're going to find on the other side of that door?" Annie asked me.

"I don't have to be. In twenty seconds, we're going to find out for ourselves."

"That's what I'm afraid of," Annie replied. It was uncharacteristic for her to be nervous about anything. I looked over to see that she was physically shaking.

"Sis, no matter how this turns out, we've got each other, and Kathleen, too. Remember that and you'll be fine."

"Okay," she said, taking a deep gulp of breath, letting it out slowly, and then reaching out and rapping at the door.

An older woman who looked remarkably like my late mother threw the door open and embraced us both at the same time. It was clear that she'd been crying just before we'd arrived. Was everyone getting overly emotional about this little reunion but me?

"Pat, Annie, it's awful, but I'm so glad you're here," she said, dabbing at her eyes.

"What's going on, Della?" I asked her. "Has something happened?"

"It's Cheryl Simmons. She's dead. Someone must have thought she was me, and they killed her."

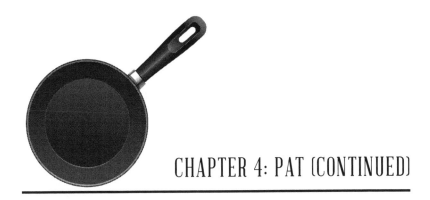

CHAPTER 4: PAT (CONTINUED)

"**H**ANG ON. SLOW DOWN AND back up a little bit," I said. "Start at the beginning."

Instead of explaining, Della began crying again in full force. "I'm starting to realize that I should never have brought you both here. It's not safe for you to be in Gateway Lake. I've risked your lives for mine, something my sister never would have forgiven me for."

"May we discuss this inside?" I asked, looking around to see a few neighbors peering out their windows, watching us all intently.

"Of course," she said. "It's just so awful, I don't know what I'm going to do."

We walked into a space that I wasn't expecting. Instead of doilies and old wallpaper, the interior was sleek and modern, though compact. Stainless steel was everywhere, and the light fixtures had a decidedly industrial tone to them. The furniture was ultramodern as well, and I hoped she had bed space for us both; the couch looked like a ready-made back killer.

"May I get you something?" Annie asked her as she guided our aunt to the sofa in question.

"Some water from the fridge would be nice," she said.

"Are you sure you wouldn't like something a little stronger?" I offered. I didn't know what her liquor situation was, but if she needed a drink of something stronger than water, I was going to go get it for her. After all, she'd just lost someone.

"No, water is all I need."

While Annie was taking care of that, I said, "Take a deep breath, and then tell us what happened to Cheryl."

"I can't get over how grown up you both look," Aunt Della replied instead of answering my question as she studied me. Then she glanced at Annie and added, "Your sister looks a great deal like her mother did at that age."

I couldn't resist, despite my earlier promise and the woman's obvious duress. "I don't know. I kind of think she looks like Dad."

"Patrick Marsh," Annie scolded me from the kitchen, proving that she'd been listening in to our conversation.

"It's all right, Annie. I can see him in her, too. I know my apology isn't worth much to you both, but I am truly sorry for the way I behaved."

"It's fine, Aunt Della," Annie said as she hurried back with the water.

"It's not, but it's sweet of you to say so," Aunt Della answered.

I refrained from commenting altogether. "Tell us about your friend."

Della took a long sip of water, and then she set it aside. "Very well."

"If you need a minute to compose yourself, we can wait," Annie said.

It took nearly all I had not to glare at my twin sister. I knew she was right, but I wanted to find out what had happened. If the murderer had indeed meant to kill our aunt, the more we knew and the faster we knew it, the better.

"She was here with me last night," Della started to explain. "I shared my concerns with her about the incidents that have been happening to me lately, and she did her best to reassure me that everything would be all right. Cheryl must have been here three hours, because by the time she left, it was dark outside, and the wind had begun to blow something fierce. There are some real benefits to living on the lake, but it isn't all sunshine and roses. I knew she would be freezing on her walk back, so I loaned her my long coat. It's quite distinctive, and everyone in town has seen me in it dozens of times."

"Funny, I didn't even see the lake on the drive in," I said.

"That's because it skirts the back of all of our properties," she explained. "You really can't see it very well from here at night, but during the day, it's spectacular. Anyway, Cheryl lives, or lived, half a mile down from me, and she must have taken the lake walk instead of going on the road. They found her body right after we spoke. I know I should have called you, but I just couldn't bring myself to do it."

"Do you happen to know how she died?" I asked.

"It's too painful for me to talk about," Della said, and I could see that she was on the edge of tears again.

I expected Annie to offer to console her instead of push on with the questioning, but to my relief, my sister said, "It's important, Aunt Della."

"All I know is that someone found her body in the water," she said. "You'd have to ask the police chief for more than that."

"Do you know him very well?" I asked.

"We dated for several months," she said. "I'd say that qualifies, even if it was ten years ago."

"Will he cooperate with us?" Annie asked.

"I doubt it. He hasn't been all that fond of me ever since I broke his heart again."

Again? What did that mean? I didn't want to get into it then and there. I had more important questions to ask her. "Is there anyone else who might be able to tell us what happened?" I asked her.

"Davis would know," she said. "He knows everything."

I doubted that were true, but if he could help us, I was all for calling him in. "Can you get him on the phone?"

"It would be easier just going next door. He bought the house next to mine three months ago," she said. "I don't know if I can bear going with you, though. Would you two mind terribly going over there without me?"

"He doesn't know us, Della," I said, again omitting the 'aunt' honorific from her name. She was going to have to earn that designation back, I decided.

"I'll call him and let him know that you're on your way," she said.

As Della went for her phone, Annie asked softly, "Are you seriously not going to call her 'aunt' the entire time that we're here?"

"Trust me, it's less complicated this way," I said.

"For you or for her?"

"Annie, I need some distance if I'm going to work on this case. Just give me this one, okay?"

She frowned a moment, and then she nodded. "Fine, but we're not finished talking about this."

"Oh, goody," I said. "I can hardly wait."

She punched my arm lightly, and then Della came back.

"He's next door. Go on over. You might want to take the front way out, though."

"Actually, the lake walk might be more helpful to us," I said.

"Pat, are you *trying* to be disagreeable?" Annie asked me.

"Don't you want to see the path that leads to where Cheryl was killed?" I asked.

"It's fine, Annie," Della said.

"Okay, I suppose that makes sense," Annie conceded. "Aunt Della, do you have a strong flashlight we could use?"

"Oh, dear. I'm sorry, but I'm afraid that I gave that to Cheryl last night when I loaned her my coat."

"That's okay. I have one in my car," my sister said. "Come on, Pat. Let's go."

I nodded as I grabbed my coat after Annie did the same with hers. My sister turned back to Della before we left and said, "Don't worry. We won't be long."

"Please don't. I'm terrified of being alone right now."

Annie patted her shoulder softly. "We'll be next door if you need us."

Evidently Cheryl hadn't been much farther away herself when she'd been murdered, but I chose not to bring that up. "Let's go," I told Annie.

It was getting colder all right. The temperature must have dropped five degrees since we'd arrived, and the wind had picked up quite a bit as well. "I can see why she needed to borrow Della's coat," I said as we walked to Annie's Subaru. My sister opened the hatchback and retrieved a long and stout-looking flashlight that would easily substitute as a cudgel.

"That should do," she said as she flipped it on and a bright beam of light suddenly appeared. "Would you like to lead the way, Pat?"

"Are you actually offering to give up control of the flashlight?" I asked her with a laugh.

"No, I wasn't really serious."

"Then why did you make the offer?" I asked as I followed her around the house to the lake path in back.

"Just think how generous I would have looked if you'd been gracious and refused," my sister said.

I chuckled, completely understanding her logic. Some folks thought Annie's sense of humor was a little off, but I'd grown up with it, so it made perfect sense to me. As we headed toward the backyard, I could see the lake or, more truthfully, a large black hole in the landscape. Maybe stars would have reflected off it if it hadn't been so overcast, but at the moment, there was only a vast span of darkness out there, swallowing up every bit of light within its reach.

Annie's flashlight beam quickly found the worn dirt path that skirted along the lake.

"Could she have tripped and fallen on one of these?" I asked as I almost did as I'd posited, narrowly avoiding taking a spill from a tree root poking up from the middle of the path.

"I don't know. I suppose that depends on how she died."

"This has to be Davis's house," Annie said as we neared the next place. There was a light on the back deck, probably turned on for us. My sister started up that way when I noticed that there were other lights coming from just around the bend.

"Keep going," I said.

"We can't do that. He's waiting for us," she protested.

"Yes, but the cops appear to still be at the crime scene. How can we not check that out? He'll wait."

Annie reluctantly started back toward me, and as we rounded the bend, I saw four police officers scouring the area. There was crime scene tape stretched around a fifty-foot perimeter, including blocking the path we were on, and if we were going to get any closer, we were going to have to climb up the bank to get to them, which was what we did. A pair of plywood snowmen paid silent vigil to the scene, and they suddenly made me uneasy, judging the scene with their painted black stares. At least all of these had been painted mostly white.

I was suddenly blinded by an intensely bright light shining in my face.

"Who goes there?" a commanding voice rang out into the night.

"It's Pat and Annie Marsh," I said as I put my hand in front of the beam, trying to stop the light from searing my retinas.

"I don't know who you are," he said suspiciously.

"We just got into town," Annie said. "We're Della Mahoney's family."

That news didn't seem to appease him at all, so maybe Della had been right in her assessment of their relationship. "It's common knowledge that she doesn't have any family. Her sister died in a car wreck a long time ago."

"That was our mother," Annie said.

Finally, the flashlight beam lowered, though I knew I wouldn't be seeing clearly again for quite some time. At the moment, all I could see was the afterimage of that blinding light. I was going to have to follow Annie to make sure that I didn't slip on the steep terrain and fall into the lake.

"What are you doing here?" he asked us as he came up to the tape, but didn't cross it.

"It's nice to meet you, Sheriff..." Annie said, extending her hand.

"It's chief, actually," he corrected her as he took it. "Chief Cameron."

"Chief, what happened? Did Cheryl Simmons drown?" I asked him after he shook my hand as well.

"That's yet to be determined," he asked as he eyed me suspiciously. "What concern is that of yours? Did you know her?"

"No, but clearly our aunt is upset about what happened to her friend," Annie said, smoothing things over. "We heard that she drowned."

The chief shook his head. "That's what you get for listening to gossip."

"Do you mean they didn't find her in the water?" Annie asked.

"I didn't say that," Chief Cameron said.

This man was clearly not a fan of sharing what he knew with strangers. Imagine that. "It might help Aunt Della to know that what happened to her friend wasn't her fault," I said.

"Why would she think that it ever was?" he asked, looking oddly at me.

"Think about it from her point of view. Cheryl Simmons left Della's place in the dark wearing our aunt's hooded jacket. Della is under the impression that someone killed Cheryl by mistake. Does that fit in with what you know so far?" I asked him.

Instead of answering, he laughed softly. "That's Della for you, all right. She wants to be the bride at every wedding and the body at every funeral. Nothing but being the center of attention would ever be enough for her."

"So then you think that someone *meant* to kill Cheryl?" Annie asked.

"And succeeded pretty well at that," he replied. After a moment, he asked, "What are *you* doing here?"

"We already told you," I said. Had the man already forgotten? Then I realized that he was talking to someone who'd crept up in the dark behind us. It was an older man with a full head of gray hair that seemed to shine on its own in the night.

"Davis, I've told you twice. I don't have any comment," the police chief said testily.

The man grinned at him for a moment, and then he answered, "Take it easy, Cam. I'm not here for you." He looked at us, each in turn. "You must be Pat and Annie."

"Guilty as charged," I said, which was my normal response, though maybe not that appropriate at the moment, given the circumstances. It was pretty clear that the police chief felt that way, anyway.

"Why don't you two come back to my place with me, and I'll make something to warm us up. You won't get anything from the chief, here, not if he doesn't want to give you the information."

"So, it's finally sinking in, is it?" Chief Cameron asked with the hint of a smile.

"I was talking to them," Davis said with a smile of his own. "Come on, you two. Let's go."

I wanted to stay and talk to the police chief a little more, but Davis was probably right. The chief wasn't exactly in a chatting mood.

"Chief, over here!" one of the deputies called out. "I think I found it."

"Found what?" Davis asked, shining his own light in the officer's direction.

"You all need to leave right now," the chief said, blocking our vision of what had just been discovered. "Unless you want to spend the night in jail."

"Would you really lock the mayor up just for doing his job?" Davis asked him.

"Try me."

Davis laughed softly and then shrugged as he turned to us. "Are you ready?"

"Let's go," Annie said.

"How did you know we were out here?" I asked him as my sister and I followed him back down the path toward his home.

"I was watching you from the window," Davis said. "There's a lot of that going on around here. Sometimes I think we live in a community of peepers."

"Did you happen to see Cheryl on her way home last night?" I asked him.

"No, sadly, I'd been up since four a.m., and by the time she took what turned out to be her last walk home, I was probably sound asleep in front of the History Channel. You know, for a station that has the word 'history' in its very name, there's not a great deal of history being broadcast on it, at least as far as I've been able to determine."

"I wouldn't know about that," I said, fighting to keep us on topic. "Do you have any information on what really happened to Cheryl Simmons?"

"I heard that you two were the real sleuths in the family, despite your sister's official status as sheriff," Davis said.

"How do you happen to know so much about us?" Annie asked him.

"You're kidding, right? Your aunt hasn't been able to stop talking about you all since she got in contact with your older sister again. Believe me, I know all about you."

"I doubt that," Annie said with a grin.

"Yes, you're probably right," he conceded. "Come on up."

"Should we all go over to Aunt Della's together instead?" Annie asked him.

I could see Davis's frown in Annie's light. "Probably not. What we have to talk about is most likely just going to upset her."

"You know something about what happened to Cheryl Simmons, don't you?" I asked him.

"Maybe," he answered. "Did Della happen to tell you anything about me?"

"Not a peep, but I've got a few guesses," I said.

Davis laughed. "I bet you do. Why am I not surprised that Della hasn't mentioned me? Well, as you might have suspected, I'm the mayor of this fair city, but that's not my full-time job. I also own and run the town's newspaper."

"Isn't that a conflict of interest?" Annie asked him.

"No, it's perfect. If there's any corruption in city hall, I'm the one who knows all about it. I can scoop the rest of the world by exposing it and facilitating my own downfall. It's kind of perfectly ironic, don't you think?"

I liked this man's wry sense of humor. "You must have the best resources in town, given both of your vocations."

"You'd think so, wouldn't you? But all I've been able to find out so far is that Cheryl was murdered between ten last night and four this afternoon."

"What are you basing that on?" Annie asked.

"It's easy. Cheryl left Della's at ten, and walkers found her body this afternoon at four. From the look of things, Cheryl must have rolled off the path into the water; whether she had help or not is yet to be determined. Given the weather we've been having lately, it's lucky that she was found when she was. If it had been someplace else, we most likely wouldn't even know that she was dead yet."

"People were out walking, even this time of year?" Annie asked. "Isn't it a bit brisk?"

"It is for me," Davis said, "but not for the Go Girls."

"I'm sorry, the Go Girls?" I asked.

"That's what we call the three women in their seventies who powerwalk that path every late afternoon. They are so reliable, you can set your watch by them. They are all widows, and they go around the lake every day together, rain or shine. The only time they don't walk is in the snow, and we haven't had much accumulation this year, at least not so far."

"That must have been a horrible discovery for them," Annie said.

"The girls are tough, and at least they had each other," Davis said. "I wonder what Cam and his people found just now."

"Is there any way you can find out?" I asked.

"Not right now, but ask me again in the morning."

"In the meantime, could we ask you some other questions about what's been going on?" I asked him.

"Sure, I'll be happy to help if I can." Before he could finish though, he got a phone call, excused himself, and then stepped away. After a few minutes of hushed conversation, he came back. "Sorry. I'm going to have to postpone this conversation until tomorrow."

"Is it about the murder?" I asked him.

Davis would only shrug. "I'm sure we'll run into each other tomorrow."

"Absolutely," Annie said, and we headed back down the path toward Della's place as Davis took off toward his own home.

"That was frustrating," I said as we made our way back to Della's.

"No worries, Pat. Like he said, we can always catch up with him tomorrow," Annie said. "For now, let's go talk to our aunt again."

"She's already said that she can't help us with Cheryl's murder case," I reminded her.

"According to her, there's a great deal more than that we can talk about," my sister said.

"Sis, I don't really want to get into family history tonight."

"I'm talking about the attempts on her life," Annie replied. "We might not be able to work on Cheryl's murder right away, but we can at least ask Della what makes her think that someone wants her dead."

CHAPTER 5: ANNIE

"Wнат тоок you вотн so long?" Aunt Della asked as she flung the door open for us. "I was about to call the police."

"We met your police chief while we were out there," Pat said.

"What? Why? How did that happen?"

"Relax, Aunt Della," I said. "Pat and I were on our way to Davis's place when we saw lights on the path. The chief and three of his staff were out searching for something."

"What were they looking for?"

"We don't know," Pat said, "but from the sound of it, they found it."

"Did Cam tell you what it was they uncovered?" our aunt asked.

Cam, was it now? I wondered if everyone in town called him that or if it had been her pet name for him. Davis had called him that as well, so maybe it didn't mean anything. Then again, maybe it did. I couldn't see the police chief and my aunt involved romantically, but then again, I knew that life threw some strange couples together. Pat and his new girlfriend were a case in point, given that she was a vet, though Timothy and I suited each other quite well, at least our lifestyle choices. "He didn't share that particular bit of information with us," I told her.

"Or much else, for that matter," Pat added. "He wasn't really all that helpful."

"I'd better phone Davis. He'll be worried sick that you didn't show up." Was there a hint of scolding in her voice as she said it? Did our aunt still think we were the children we'd been when she'd last seen us?

I wasn't about to put up with that, and I knew without a doubt that Pat wouldn't, either.

"Della, relax," Pat said amiably.

"We saw him, too, while we were out there," I quickly added. "Davis is kind of nice, isn't he?"

"The truth is, he's been sweet on me for some time now," our aunt said.

Seriously? Maybe the police chief had been right about Aunt Della after all. First our aunt had told us that she'd dated the police chief once upon a time, and now, apparently the mayor was in love with her. "Why wouldn't he be?" I asked, giving my voice a hint of sarcasm.

She took it as a compliment, but Pat grinned at me discreetly.

"I'll have you know that I am considered quite the catch in some circles," Aunt Della said.

"No doubt. Could we talk about what's been happening in your life that has you so worried?" I asked before she could tell us that someone else was secretly in love with her as well.

"I told you, Davis knows everything. Didn't he share *anything* with you?"

"He was called away abruptly before we could talk much," Pat said. "But what we need now we can't get from him."

"I told you earlier, I don't know anything about what happened to Cheryl," Aunt Della said with a frown.

"That's not what we need right now," my twin brother said patiently. "We need to hear what led you to call Kathleen in the first place." Pat hadn't meant any judgment by his statement; I could hear that much in his voice, but evidently our aunt took it otherwise.

"Patrick, are you still upset that I reached out to your older sister instead of either one of you?" Della asked.

My brother shook his head. "Della, I'm sorry if you're feeling guilty about not contacting Annie or me earlier, but I'm not judging you on what you did before. As far as I'm concerned, we're starting out with a clean slate here. At least that's my intention." I could see his frustration building, and I couldn't really blame him. The woman may have been family, but she was beginning to drive me crazy. I could only imagine how Pat must have been feeling.

It was time to get her back on the subject. "You said that you were in fear for your life. Why?" I asked.

"I don't like talking about it," Aunt Della said, biting her lower lip after she said it.

"I realize that it can't be pleasant for you, but we need to know the details if we stand any chance of helping you," I said.

"I suppose I don't have any choice, do I?" she asked. "Would you like some coffee before we get started? I need some myself."

I could see that Pat was about to prod her again, but I knew that we had to let Della tell us what we were wanting to know at her own pace, or we'd never get anything out of her.

"That sounds lovely," I said as I followed her into the kitchen.

"Seriously?" Pat whispered to me.

All I could do was shrug.

"I have some cookies I bought at the Winter Wonderland yesterday," Aunt Della said as she reached into the cabinet and brought out a brightly wrapped paper plate of snowflake cookies and gingerbread snowmen.

"We saw the signs for that coming in," I said, trying to make conversation to ease her into talking to us. "Was it fun?"

"I thought it would be at first, but if I knew how much work it would be to act as co-chair of it all, I never would have let Henrietta talk me into it in the first place."

"You mean to say that you helped run the whole thing?" I asked.

"It was a great deal of work, but it was all done for a good cause. The local school system's budget has been slashed by the state again, and we decided to raise money to help out in whatever way we can."

"Was it a success?" Pat asked as he nibbled at a snowman. I knew that was the one he would go for; my brother had a weakness for gingerbread that bordered on obsession.

"We won't know until Henrietta and I get around to tallying up the final receipts and paying our expenses. Not everyone was kind enough to donate their services, so we had to cover quite a few costs. Henrietta's in charge of all that, so I really don't have a clue as to where we stand at the moment, but I'm hopeful."

I could see that Pat was finished with the small talk. Him biting off the snowman's head was a pretty good sign that he was getting more frustrated with the situation by the minute.

"Aunt Della, how did someone try to kill you?" I asked her.

She sighed heavily, but it must have been clear to her that we weren't going to be put off any longer. "Three days ago, I was inspecting the parade route on First Avenue. They call it Freedom Lane now, but it will always be First Avenue to me. Anyway, I was standing in front of the bank trying to see if there would be enough room for the bystanders and the floats we'd be having when something fell off the roof and nearly split my head wide open right there on the sidewalk."

"What fell?" Pat asked her, suddenly losing all interest in the snowman he'd been eating so intently just a second earlier.

"It was one of the snowmen from the roof," she said. "It landed within four feet of me, and I have to say, if it had been a direct hit, I wouldn't be here with you both right now."

"A snowman?" Pat asked her.

"Like the ones we saw in town, I'll bet, not one really made of snow. It was plywood, right?" I asked her.

"Of course it was made of wood. Did you see any snow on your drive in?"

"Is there any chance the falling snowman might have been an accident?" I asked her. "You said yourself that it's been awfully windy lately."

"That's what Riley Jenkins, the contractor who was in charge of putting them up everywhere, kept trying to say, but I know better. Things just don't fall from the sky for no reason, even if no one was supposed to be up there when it happened. What I want to know is what made that particular snowman fall at the precise moment that I was standing directly beneath it?"

"Actually, you weren't. If you had been, it would have hit you on the head, and you wouldn't have been in any condition to talk to us right now," Pat reminded her.

"It very well could have, if my reactions hadn't been so finely honed after years of doing yoga three nights a week at the rec center."

I didn't even know how to respond to that. "What else has happened? Surely one incident isn't enough to cause so much alarm," I said.

"Then there was the parade itself. I was making my way through the crowd to be sure that everything went off without a hitch when someone shoved me in the back out into the path of the fire truck. I could have easily been killed right then and there, and there's no way you can possibly write that off as mere coincidence."

"Maybe, maybe not. You said that this happened during the parade. Exactly how fast was the fire truck going?" Pat asked her.

"Not very," she conceded, "but given the way that it happened, I could have been crushed before anyone actually knew what was happening. If it hadn't been for Davis next door, I would be dead yet again."

"What does the mayor have to do with you escaping harm?" I asked her.

"Why, he's the one who reached out and pulled me back from the brink of death," Aunt Della said.

"That's two. Are there any more?" Pat asked.

"Do you mean besides the fact that someone killed my best friend coming home from visiting me while wearing my coat? I've got to say, I don't care for your questions, young man."

"Aunt Della, you asked us for our help, remember?" Pat was keeping his cool, and I was proud of him for doing it. "We're just trying to figure out what really happened."

"It's all part of the process," I said. "Now, did anything else happen?"

"Besides being nearly poisoned to death, you mean?" she asked petulantly. "Does that count?"

"Tell us what happened," Pat said.

"At the town supper after the parade, I grew desperately sick from something I ate. It became immediately obvious that I had been poisoned by someone intending to harm me."

"Hang on a second," I said, beating Pat to the punch. "How do you know that?"

"It's simple. No one else was sick from the food but me," she said.

"I'm not trying to imply anything, but you don't *look* sick," Pat said.

"Are you doubting me?" she asked him.

"No, ma'am. I'm just saying that you recovered pretty quickly, if this all just happened yesterday evening," he said.

"What can I say? I'm a quick healer. I always have been. Whatever I ingested was meant to kill me, though. I had to run to the ladies room before I embarrassed myself, and when I got back, someone had removed the evidence. My plate was gone, so I can't even prove that I was poisoned."

I imagined that any unclaimed plate of food would be tossed in order to keep the place clean, but I wasn't about to bring that up.

"So you see," Aunt Della said, "None of this was simply in my mind. That plywood fell near me, I was nearly pushed under the fire truck, I barely escaped dying of poison, and when none of those things worked, someone killed my best friend, thinking it was me."

"Did you share all of this with anyone else?" Pat asked.

"Who else would I tell?" she asked.

"The police chief, the mayor, even Henrietta, just to name a few," Pat said. "We need to know who else is aware of what has been happening to you."

"I've kept it all to myself. I trust only my family at a time like this," she said sternly. "I thought I could count on you."

Why on earth did she think that, after such a long absence on her part? I could see Pat gearing up for a rebuttal when I cut him off. "Okay, if that's it, we've got the basics down now. Let us look around town, ask a few questions, and see what we can find out," I said as I started to stand up.

"When, tonight?" she asked, clearly frightened by the prospect of being alone again.

"We're not deserting you, but it has to be tonight," Pat said. "The sooner we get started, the better."

"Please don't leave me," she pled.

"Be reasonable, Aunt Della. How can we help you if we don't talk to some of the folks who might want to wish you harm?"

"Surely it can wait until tomorrow," she said as she moved to the coffee pot, where the brew was now complete. As Della filled three mugs, she said, "Besides, I was hoping we could take this time to catch up and get reacquainted."

"If we stay, we need to spend the time talking more about your situation," Pat said firmly.

"I've told you everything I know, and that's the truth."

"Not everything, I'm afraid," Pat said, keeping his voice easy.

Aunt Della looked shocked by the statement. "What could I have possibly left out?"

I knew the answer to that without having to defer to my brother. "You haven't told us why anyone would want to see you dead. It's been our experience that uncovering the motive is critical in solving the crime." I'd only just managed to stop myself from saying the word "murder." I was afraid how our aunt would react to that.

"I don't know why *anyone* would want to kill me," she said, and I honestly believed her. That didn't help us out any.

"Think hard," Pat said as he sipped his coffee. "Have you enraged anyone lately? Do you know anyone else's secrets? Have you slept with someone else's husband, by any chance? Something like that would be a real help."

"Young man, you need to take that back right now," Aunt Della said angrily.

"It's a fair question," Pat said as he shrugged.

"Annie, are you going to let him get away with that? Surely you were both raised better than that."

She must have lost her mind if she thought I would ever take her side against my brother's. Even Kathleen knew enough never to try to play that card. I was loyal to Pat without fail and without question. "Coming from your nephew, I'm sure it's a little unsettling to hear, but that's not why we're here. We're investigating attempted murder, so the gloves have to come off. This is not the time to sugarcoat or obfuscate anything, Aunt Della. If there are any skeletons in your closet, it's time to trot them out into the light. If you're uncomfortable doing that with us, then I'm afraid that we're wasting our time here. Pat?"

"I agree," my brother said. "I'm not trying to offend you. I'm just looking for something that might help us stop this before it happens."

After a few moments of silence that seemed to go on forever, Aunt Della said, "I'm sorry. I overreacted, didn't I?"

Pat was gracious enough to say, "It's only natural, but we really don't mean anything by it. We're here to help, not to embarrass you."

"Very well. I'll tell you both everything, not that there's all that much to tell."

"Just start telling us about your problems, and let us be the judge of that," Pat said.

I wasn't sure what she was about to say, but I had a feeling that I wouldn't be any more comfortable hearing it than Aunt Della was in saying it, so I braced myself for my aunt's deepest and darkest secrets.

CHAPTER 6: ANNIE (CONTINUED)

"I DON'T EVEN KNOW WHERE TO begin," Aunt Della said in frustration after a few moments. "I can't think of *any* reason anyone would want to kill me."

"Don't think of it that way," I said.

"How else should she think of it?" Pat asked me. "Annie, we both know that we need a motive, unless you believe that these are just random acts of some deranged madman."

"Does that mean that you believe me?" Aunt Della asked my brother.

"I'm working on the premise that everything you've told us is true," Pat said without much inflection in his voice. It was far from an admission that he gave any credence at all to her stories, but evidently it was enough for her.

"I'm so relieved," she said.

"Now think, Aunt Della," I said. "Don't worry about being outlandish or be concerned about besmirching someone else's name. You're among family right now, so we'll hold whatever you tell us in full confidence." I turned to look at my brother. "Right, Pat?"

"If we can do it without jeopardizing our investigation, I'll be happy to agree to that," he said.

"He's right, Aunt Della. I'm afraid that's the best we can promise," I said, agreeing with my brother. It was a foolish time to make promises that we might not be able to keep. "Can you accept that?"

"Of course. I trust you both with my life. After all, I asked you here in the first place, didn't I?"

I wasn't sure why she was ready to put her faith in the two of us, since for all intents and purposes we'd just met. "Good. I know it's going to be painful for you, but we're asking you these questions for a reason. If we know who might want to wish you ill, then we can focus on a particular set of suspects instead of just going around town accusing everyone we happen to run into."

"I can see your point there," she said with a whisper of a smile.

Taking a deep breath and then letting it out slowly, she finally began to answer the most pressing question we'd posed for her so far. "First of all, I don't know how you can live very long in this world without making enemies. Over the course of the past fifty-plus years, I've probably made more than my share. I'm a woman of strong opinions, and a great many folks don't like that."

"We're not asking you for a general rendition of your past sins and shortcomings," Pat said with a smile. "We need specifics, Della."

"It's hard to say. Maybe it's a heart I've broken. That would include Cam and a few other men in town. None of them were happy when I dumped them, but I can't see any of them wanting to see me dead. This is really difficult."

"Okay, we'll deal with your distant exes later. Is there anyone you've dumped recently?" I asked her.

"Annie, I've been good for quite a while. The last serious interest I sparked would have to be Davis, and I'm not at all sure how intent he was when he asked me out the last time."

"What do you mean, the last time?" Pat asked.

"Davis has been after me for a date for six months, but I keep turning him down."

"Why?" I asked. "He seems like a nice guy."

"He is, but it's not that easy. First of all, I'm not sure I want to date *anyone* right now, including him, but even if I did, I'd have second thoughts about trying to go through Serena Jefferson to get to him."

"Who is Serena?" Pat asked her as he started taking notes on a piece of paper. It was a good idea, since I had a hunch we were going to need a scorecard before this investigation was over.

"She's his secretary, and believe me, that woman believes she owns the mayor, and anyone else who even gets close to him is in for a hard time of it."

"Have they ever dated?" I asked her.

"No, not that she doesn't dream about it every night before she goes to sleep. She's in love with him, that much is clear to anyone who's ever been around the two of them together, but as a woman, Davis doesn't even know that she exists."

"Do you honestly believe that she might be trying to do away with you to clear the path for her own run at him?" I asked her.

"You should see the woman's eyes. She's a little crazy when it comes to her boss."

"Could Davis be upset with your constant rejections?" Pat asked. Was he buying into her story or just being thorough? Aunt Della was an attractive woman, there was no doubt about that, but she certainly wasn't one of the all-time great beauties of our century.

"I suppose it's possible," she said.

"I would think there was a case to be made for it. After all, he did buy the house right beside yours. That sounds a little obsessive to me."

"It wasn't like that," Aunt Della explained. "The house came on the market suddenly, and the mayor has always wanted to live on the water. Him buying that house has nothing to do with me."

"Can you be sure of that?" I asked her.

"I suppose anything's possible," Aunt Della answered. "So, that's three people on our list already, if we include the police chief."

"When we mentioned your name to him earlier, he seemed irritated with you more than anything else," Pat answered.

"Well, the line between love and hate is a fine one indeed," Aunt Della said.

"Has he asked you out recently?" I wanted to know.

"Yes, but it won't happen again anytime soon. I crushed his hopes quite soundly the last time he asked me."

"When was that?"

"As a matter of fact, it was right before the Winter Wonderland festivities all started," she said, and then she frowned for a moment in thought afterward. "At first, I thought he was joking about asking me to the town supper where I ended up being poisoned, so I laughed it off. It wasn't until later that I realized that he must have been serious. It's no wonder the man's not very happy with me at the moment."

"Does that cover all of your recent romantic rejections?" Pat asked.

"I would think so," she replied.

"Okay then, what other motives might someone have to want to see you dead?" he asked.

"It's a disturbing thing to think about, isn't it?"

"Aunt Della, it's the only way we have to figure out what's going on with you," I said. "Think hard. Don't hold anything back."

"Well, there is one thing. I was in the dressing room at Starland's last week—it's a women's clothing store here in town—and I overheard something troubling."

"What did you hear?" I asked.

"Two women were discussing doing away with someone while I was changing," she said. "It sounded as though they were trying to get rid of someone to me."

"Do you have any idea who was talking?" Pat asked intently.

"No, I'm afraid not. You see, the zipper on the dress I was trying on was stuck, and it took me ten minutes to get it undone. By the time I got out of the dressing room, they were both gone."

"Is there any chance they knew that you were there?" I asked her.

Aunt Della frowned. "Yes, I'm afraid so. Cindy Nance, the young lady who was working the sales floor that day, asked me if I needed any help right after I overheard them plotting. I'm afraid they knew I was there, all right."

That could be trouble. If Aunt Della knew something, or if a pair of would-be killers even thought she knew their plans, it could spell trouble for her. "We need to talk to Cindy. Is there any chance you asked her who was there at the store when you were?"

"I didn't want to bring any more attention to myself than I already had," she admitted. "I'm afraid that zipper was broken beyond repair, and I wanted her to forget that I'd even been there trying anything on. It was poorly made, but I didn't want to have to pay for shoddy material. Should I have told her about it?"

Pat rolled his eyes a little as I said, "I'm sure that it's fine. You said that you've been involved with the Winter Wonderland festivities. Could you have slighted someone in your preparations for that?"

"Annie, I denied a few vendors booth space, but it would hardly be a motive for murder."

"Okay then, did you have any arguments with anyone over the way you and Henrietta were running things?"

"Gary White," she said gravely. "He was pretty upset with what we decided."

"Tell us about it."

"He wanted us to run the parade route past his hardware store, but we chose to go by the bank instead. There wouldn't have been enough room for the floats to get through if we'd done what he wanted, but would he listen to reason? He would not. I'm afraid it got a bit ugly. He said that he'd rather see the entire festivities go up in flames than let it go on without him. My elimination would have surely accomplished that, wouldn't it have?"

I made a mental note to speak with Gary White as I saw Pat jotting the name down on his paper. Great minds thought alike. "Is there anyone else?"

"No, not that I can think of. That's surely enough, isn't it?" She looked drained from the experience, something that I understood. After all, it couldn't be easy trying to think of folks who might want to kill you.

"It will do for a start," Pat said.

"Is that all, then?" she asked us.

"Sorry, but that just covers you," my brother told her. "We need to talk about Cheryl Simmons now, if you're up for it."

"Why do we need to discuss poor Cheryl?" she asked, her voice starting to whine.

"Aunt Della, what if she weren't killed by accident? If someone wanted her dead, shouldn't we look into that as well?" I asked her.

"Can't Cam do that? Surely he's better equipped to investigate what happened to her than you two are. No offense."

"None taken," Pat said automatically. "So, if it's really a case of mistaken identity, then her murder is pertinent to your case, but if she was killed for other reasons, then you're fine with letting the police handle things."

"You make it sound so cold and callous when you put it that way," Aunt Della said.

"We're just trying to make the best use of our time and resources," I reassured her, even though I thought Pat's summation of her beliefs was spot on. "We have only four days, you know."

"Can't you possibly stay longer?" she asked in a soft whimper.

"Sorry, but we're stretching things as it is," I replied. "If we can't help over the course of the next few days, we're most likely not going to be able to help at all."

"Today counts as well, then?" she asked incredulously.

"I'm sorry, but it has to," I said, and Pat nodded in silent agreement. I knew the odds were good that we wouldn't be able to solve this, especially given such a limited amount of time, but we really had no choice. Leaving the Iron in other people's hands, no matter how suited they may have been to act in our steads, was something that we were not willing to do any longer than was absolutely necessary, and the sooner Aunt Della accepted that fact, the better for all of us.

CHAPTER 7: PAT

I T TURNED OUT THAT I had been right about the sleeping arrangements.

Aunt Della brought me sheets, a blanket, and a pillow. "I'm sorry about the couch, but I have only one guest room, and it's pink. You don't mind sleeping out here, do you?"

"No, I'm sure this will be fine," I said as I took the bedding from her. Behind our aunt, I saw Annie stick her tongue out at me, and it took all I had not to laugh.

Della must have seen something though, and she misinterpreted the expression on my face. "Pat, I know how hard this is for you, and I want to thank you for coming. It's clear that you're not happy with me, and the truth of that matter is that I don't blame you. I've made so many mistakes over the years. I wish I had it all to do over again, but that's not an option, is it? The best I can do is try to make up for lost time. Will you give me that opportunity?"

"Della, all I can say is that I'm doing the best that I can. I'm not trying to hurt you. It's just hard for me, you know?" I answered honestly. "Let's figure out what's really going on here, and then we'll deal with our family issues. Does that sound fair to you?"

"Perfectly. By the way, I'm fine with you just calling me Della. After all, you're a little old to call me aunt, aren't you?"

"It just makes things seem a little less complicated," I said. "There is no disrespect intended by it."

"You know, you have some of your mother in you," she said.

"How do you mean?"

47

"She was never afraid to say exactly what she meant, no matter the consequences. It was one of the things I admired most about her, actually. I miss her."

"I do, too, and my father as well," I said. There was no criticism in my statement, and she must have sensed that it had been a benign comment, given that she didn't react to it.

"I'm sure that you do. If you need anything, I'm in the other room."

"I'll be fine," I said.

"Coming, Annie?" she asked as she turned to my sister, who was still standing right behind her.

"In a minute," she said. "I want to talk to Pat for a minute first."

"Very well. Good night, twins."

We both said our good night simultaneously, something that made Della smile.

"Are you okay out here?" Annie asked as she helped me make up the couch.

"I'll manage. I hope you enjoy your big comfy bed while I'm out here suffering on this atrocity."

"You saw that room. It looks as though a bottle of Pepto-Bismol blew up in there. I've never seen so much pink in my entire life."

"Want to trade?" I asked her with a smile.

"No, I have a feeling that the pink won't bother me nearly so much once my eyes are closed. Do we have a solid plan for the morning?"

"Well, one thing's for sure. We can't stay here and babysit our aunt all day. We need to get out amongst the townsfolk and see what we can find out."

"I spotted a diner on the way into town," Annie offered. "That might be a good place to start."

"Why am I not surprised you'd find a grill to check out while we were here?" I asked her with a grin.

"Pat, you know as well as I do that a small-town life revolves around

48

food. We've got a better chance of finding out what's really going on by visiting there than we do camping out on the police chief's front steps."

"I can't argue with you there. Annie, do you believe Della?"

"What, her theories about who might want to see her dead?" my sister asked me softly.

"Not just that, but the fact that it appears that all of the men in town over fifty consider her an object of obsessive desire, at least according to her," I answered.

"Be nice," she said as she swatted at me.

"Sorry. I couldn't help myself." I stretched out on the couch once we made it up, and to my surprise, though it hadn't been all that comfortable to sit on, it made a shockingly adequate bed. I wouldn't trade it for my own spot back home above the Iron, but it would do in a pinch, and as a bonus, I didn't have to deal with the pink nightmare that Annie faced every time she opened her eyes.

"You're really trying with her, aren't you? I'm proud of you, Pat."

"Thanks. I'm glad you noticed," I said with a smile.

She patted me on the head, and then she said, "I'll let you get some sleep. See you in the morning."

"Not if I see you first," I said, a childish response that we still used occasionally. We might not be kids anymore, but in certain ways, we'd never really grown up, which suited me just fine.

It was an uneasy sleep, due more to the fact that I was not at home in my own bed than the fact that I was on my aunt's couch. I seemed to wake up every ten minutes, and I'd just gotten back to sleep sometime around two a.m. when I heard someone scrambling around on the front porch. The cottage was a creaky old beast, and the footsteps outside were hard to hide. I sat up from the couch and looked at the front door just as the handle started to jiggle a little. Had we locked the place up before bed? I'd just assumed that Della had taken care of it, but now I wasn't so sure. I got up from the couch and made my way to the door, grabbing a lamp along the way after jerking the plug from the wall. It was a testament to my aunt's love of all things modern, full of gleaming, sharp angles, but I didn't have any problem with it at the moment, since the base had been fashioned from a large hunk of polished steel. It had a good heft to it, and I wasn't afraid to use it.

"Who's there?" I asked loudly as I tried to find the light switch that controlled the porch lights. Instead of finding that one, though, I managed to turn the overhead living room lights on, instantly killing my night vision. After another failed attempt, I found the right switch and flicked it on as I peered outside.

Whoever had been there was now gone.

———◦✦◦———

I was just about to open the front door to investigate further when Annie and Della came into the room.

"What's going on, Pat?" my sister asked.

"Someone was outside," I said.

"It was probably just the wind," my aunt said. "This place makes more noise than a bagful of badgers when a stiff wind is blowing."

"The doorknob started turning, and I haven't seen the wind that will do that," I said. "You both need to stay right here while I check this out."

"Come on, Pat. We both know that's not happening," Annie said as she hurried to join me.

"Both of you need to stay inside right now," Della commanded. "I'm going to call Cam."

"I wouldn't if I were you, but you can go ahead and do what you want to," I said, ignoring her earlier demand to stay right where I was. I unlocked the door and stepped outside, still carrying the lamp in my free hand. It was freezing, and I instantly regretted not grabbing my coat and shoes first.

"Trying to shed a little light on the situation?" Annie asked as we both realized that whoever had been outside was now long gone.

"It was the closest thing I had to a weapon," I acknowledged as my teeth began to chatter. "Let's go back inside. I didn't just dream that, Annie. Someone really was trying to break in."

"I never doubted you for a moment. Is break-in the right term? You said they tried the doorknob."

"Okay, but criminal trespass doesn't sound nearly as dramatic, does it?"

"Come on, little brother," she urged me. I was getting colder by the second, and she must have been as well.

I made doubly sure that the door was locked before I joined Annie and Della in the kitchen.

"When will the police chief get here?" I asked her.

"I didn't think you wanted me to call him," she said. "Should I phone him now?"

"No, I don't think it will do us any good now, and it might hurt our credibility if we need him for something else later," I said. "Thanks for taking my advice."

"It would be silly not to, given the fact that I brought you both here to help me," Della said, and then she stifled a yawn. "Is it safe to go back to bed, or should I make another pot of coffee?"

"If I drink any more caffeine tonight, I'll *never* get back to sleep," Annie said, and then she turned to me. "Pat, what do you think?"

"I believe the danger is past for tonight," I said. "Della, do you always lock the front door before you turn in for the night?"

"It's such a sleepy little town, most nights I forget to do it completely. It's not just me, though. Most folks leave their doors unlocked around here."

"I doubt many did after Cheryl Simmons was murdered," I said. "Do me a favor. From now on, make sure that everything's locked up tight before you go to bed or even leave the house during the daytime."

"Should I check the front door now, or did you lock it behind you?"

"I locked it," I admitted, "but it wouldn't hurt to get in the habit anyway."

She did as I asked and checked the door again. Nodding in satisfaction, she turned to me and said, "All secure."

"How about the back door? Does this place have a basement, and if so, does it have its own access to the outside? Are all of the windows locked, first floor and second as well?" I asked her, peppering the questions at her in rapid fire before she had a chance to respond to the first inquiry.

"I don't know," she said hurriedly. Was she about to start crying again? Had I been too tough on her, or was she just being overly sensitive? I couldn't really blame her if she were. After all, whether it was true or not, Della believed that someone was trying to kill her, and they'd struck down her best friend as well. Why wouldn't she be a little edgy about the situation?

"No worries. We'll all check them right now," Annie suggested before I could. "Why don't you take the first floor, Aunt Della? I'll check the upstairs windows, and Pat can have the basement."

Oh, boy. I wasn't all that thrilled with the idea of going down there alone, but it needed to be done. I found the light switch at the head of the stairs and made my way down. The basement lacked any charm at all, and it appeared that my aunt had decided to use the area to store anything that didn't go with her upstairs décor. It looked as though a flea market had exploded down there, and I had to make my way through thin aisles to get to the rear door and the lone window.

They had both been unlocked.

As I latched and locked them tight, I kept feeling eyes peering at me from the clutter inside, and I didn't quite run up the stairs, but it was close enough to it to count. Once I was on the main floor again, I locked the door leading down there as a secondary precaution.

When I turned around, Annie was standing there grinning at me. "How'd it go?"

"Fine. Everything's locked up tight now. How about upstairs?"

"We're all set," she said. "Della decided to go back to bed, but if you want me to help stand watch, I'll take a shift."

"No, I meant what I said. We should be good, at least for tonight,"

I said. "If whoever tried to get in stuck around any length of time at all, they'll know that we're here, and we're ready for them."

"Pat, do you really think it was someone coming for Della? Could she be right about what's been happening around here lately?"

"It's looking more and more like it to me," I admitted. "I'm not sure exactly why it's happening, but something is definitely going on."

"Don't worry. We'll figure it out. Would you like to take the pink bedroom for the rest of the night? I don't mind sleeping down here."

Her offer was sweet, but there was no way I was going to put my sister in jeopardy just because I wanted a comfortable place to sleep. "I'm good, but thanks for the offer." I hesitated a second, and then I asked her, "That offer wasn't like the flashlight thing before, was it?"

"No, this time I meant it," she said.

"Thanks, but I'm happy with the way things are."

"I'll go, but you have to make me a promise first. If you see or hear anything else, come get me before you decide to do anything stupid. Agreed?"

"If there's time for it, sure, but what if I don't have a chance? I may have to react immediately if something else happens."

She thought about that for a few seconds. "Okay, I suppose that would be all right. Just don't go getting yourself hurt, or something even worse."

"I'll do my best not to," I said, trying to force a grin that I didn't feel. "Now go to bed. We've got a big day ahead of us tomorrow, and we need what little sleep we have a chance to get now."

"I'm not sure I'll be able to nod off, but I'm willing to try if you are."

After Annie was back upstairs, I toyed with the idea of staying awake in case I was wrong about our surprise guest coming back, but the only purpose that would serve would be to deprive me of some much-needed sleep. I went into the kitchen and grabbed a few glasses from the pantry. After stacking them in front of the front door, I decided that if anyone tried to get in again, the glasses would fall and serve as an alarm. I doubted that any fictional detective would create such a haphazard alarm system, but I was tired, it was late, and morning would be arriving much too soon for my taste. It would just have to do, but I made a mental note to take them down before the women got up. Just because I was a little spooked, there was no reason to share my fears with them.

It must have helped, as little a measure as it was, because to my surprise, I managed to fall back asleep fairly quickly, and I didn't wake up again until I felt someone's presence looming over me where I slept.

CHAPTER 8: ANNIE

"**G**LASSES? REALLY? PLEASE TELL ME that you got thirsty last night and decided to get a couple of drinks of water," I said as I grinned down at my brother, holding his primitive burglar alarm system in my hands.

"It was the best I could do, given the situation," Pat admitted.

"Actually, it's kind of clever," I said. "I would have moved the chair in front of the door if I'd been sleeping down here, so you're braver than I was."

"I doubt that," he said as he stood and stretched. "I can't believe I fell back asleep. How about you? Did you have any luck?"

"Amazingly, yes. Has Aunt Della been downstairs yet?"

"How would I know? You woke me up, remember?"

"Pat, could something have happened to her last night?" I hadn't even considered the possibility that whoever had tried to visit us the night before would really come back, but now I was getting worried. I headed for the stairs, with Pat close on my heels.

We nearly collided with Della as she came out of her room, dressed for the day and clearly perplexed by our behavior. "What's going on?"

"Nothing," I said.

She didn't quite buy that. Was there a grin on her face as she asked, "You were worried about me, weren't you?"

"Okay, I admit it," I said. "So, why would that make you smile, given the circumstances?"

"It's been quite some time since anyone's been concerned about my welfare. Is it my fault that I like the feeling?"

"Of course not," I said.

"What would you two like for breakfast?" she asked us as we all made our way back down the stairs.

"I'm really sorry, but we can't eat with you," Pat said.

"What? Why not? You have to eat something," Della protested.

"We're going to the diner downtown," Pat said. "I think it's called Moe's."

"I'm perfectly capable of making you something better than you'll get there," our aunt protested. "What kind of hostess, let alone aunt, would I be to send you down there for your meals?"

"Do I need to remind you that we aren't here for the food, or the company?" Pat asked her gently. "Annie and I need to get the lay of the land, and the best way for us to do that is to have breakfast at the diner."

"Very well. I suppose it sounds like fun at that, but I'm getting the check. I understand their waffles are quite good."

I didn't want to make Pat be the one who had to tell her that she couldn't join us, so I spoke up first. "Aunt Della, nobody's going to talk to us if you're sitting there with us."

"Of course they will," she said. "That's utter nonsense."

"They'll talk," Pat agreed, "but not about the case. We've done this before, remember? That's why you asked us for our help. You're going to have to just trust us."

"I do. Of course I do."

"Then we'll see you later," Pat said. "I need to get dressed, and then we're off."

Pat grabbed his bag and went into the powder room on the first floor. Since I'd already changed, I was already ready to go.

"Your brother is not my biggest fan, is he?" Della asked me after he was out of the room.

"You have to admit that it's a lot to take in at one time," I said, making excuses for my brother, a habit that we'd both acquired over the years. "He's trying really hard, though. You need to cut him some slack."

"You don't seem to be having any problems with the situation," she said to me.

"Why, because I'm the only one who's calling you 'Aunt Della' at the moment? Don't kid yourself. I'm as thrown off by this situation as my brother is. We just have very different ways of showing it."

Della nodded. "I don't know why I'm surprised. You two always did stick up for each other, even as toddlers."

"It's what we do," I agreed. "I hope you don't mind staying here while we go out investigating."

"Do you mean that I'm restricted to the house?" she asked, clearly unhappy with that prospect.

"Della, someone's trying to kill you. Don't you think it would be prudent to keep a low profile until Pat and I have had a chance to look around first?"

"Aunt Della," she reminded me.

"Maybe Pat is right. When I call you 'aunt,' you aren't nearly as cooperative," I said with a smile to ease the sting of my words.

"What if we use my presence to flush the killer out into the open?" she asked. "That would work, wouldn't it? I can be the bait in your trap."

"You've been watching too many detective shows on television," I replied.

"Is the idea really that bad?"

"No, but we're not going to try anything like that unless things get really desperate. I'm not about to risk your life foolishly. I know it's not glamorous, but for the next few days, you need to stay right where you are and let my brother and me figure this out."

"What if whoever tried to break in this morning comes back while you're gone?" she asked me, letting a little of the fear she must be feeling through in her voice.

"Do you have any way of protecting yourself here?" I asked her.

"You mean like a gun? Of course not."

I wasn't all that surprised, but she had to have something she could use in self-defense, if only to make her feel more comfortable while we were gone. "How about a baseball bat?"

"I don't do sports," she said diffidently.

"Let me poke around downstairs while Pat's getting ready and see what I can come up with."

"I'll come with you," she said. "It's quite a mess down there."

I unlocked the door, flipped the light switch on, and started down the stairs. This place was creepy in the daytime. Pat had been braver than I'd realized going down there by himself the night before in the darkness.

I looked around at the jumble of things as Aunt Della said, "Sorry about the mess. I keep promising myself that I'll clean this up someday, but the piles seem to get higher each year."

"I get it," I said, though I'd never be able to live like that, even if my tiny cabin in the woods had a fraction of the storage my aunt's place had. I saw a thick wooden dowel leaning against an old pedal sewing machine, and I grabbed it. It was about four feet long and at least two inches thick, and I wondered if it had been used as a closet rod at some point. "This will do."

"What am I supposed to do with that?" she asked unhappily.

"I'd say swing for the fences," I answered with a grin.

My humor was lost on her. It was my own fault; she'd warned me that she wasn't a sports fan, so the baseball reference was completely lost on her. "Use it to defend yourself if anyone tries to get you. Which they won't. I promise."

Della took the rod from me as she cranked one eyebrow upward. "How exactly can you make a promise like that?"

"Okay, I can't guarantee anything. I'm just trying to make you feel better. How am I doing?"

"Let's go back upstairs, shall we?" she suggested, ignoring my question completely.

I was all for getting out of there.

Pat was waiting for us just outside the basement door when we walked out into the hallway. "There you are. I thought you two might have deserted me."

"We were just arming Aunt Della," I explained.

He looked at the heavy wooden dowel in her hands and nodded. "That should work."

"I'm not at all sure that I like this," Della said.

"We can look for something else you could use as a weapon, if you'd prefer," I said.

"I'm not talking about that. I mean the idea of you two walking around town asking questions about me."

"First of all, the questions aren't going to primarily be about you, and second, if we can't make inquiries, then why are we here?" Pat asked.

"Oh, very well. Just be careful, will you?"

"We'll do our best, but we can't make any promises," I said as Pat and I grabbed our jackets and headed out on foot into the crisp morning air toward the diner.

It was time to get something to eat, but more importantly, we needed to start digging around our aunt's life, no matter what Pat had just told her. Motive was the key to this puzzle, and without uncovering it, we'd just be spinning our wheels on the ice.

"Welcome to Moe's," a thin waitress in her forties greeted us as Pat and I walked into the worn-out diner. Her name tag pegged her as Regina, but I wasn't about to call her by name. She probably got enough tag reading as it was. The place was three quarters full at the moment, and just like home, there was a wide array of hats perched on the heads of nearly all of the men eating there. Advertising everything from tractors to sports teams, the caps made me miss my own grill back home. The colorful caps had always reminded me of peacocks, strutting their colors for all to see. The diner's ratio at the moment was probably four men for every woman present, and everybody in the place had a cup of coffee in front of them.

"Hi, Regina," Pat said with a broad smile. She didn't react to it with anything more than a "hey."

"You can sit anywhere that's not already taken," she said. "Need menus?"

"That would be great," I said as I reached for them. I started to sit at the counter, but Pat tapped my shoulder. "How about over there?" He pointed to a spot near the front window where we could hear what was going on around us without being directly involved in any of the conversations.

"Sure, that's fine," I said.

Regina was there in short order, and without even being asked, she flipped our coffee cups over and filled them to the brim. "What can I get you?"

"Two eggs, over medium, bacon not crispy, scattered hash browns that are, and two pieces of buttered white toast," Pat said.

"Ma'am?" she asked after jotting my brother's most specific order down on her pad.

"How's the oatmeal?" I asked her.

"We don't get too many complaints," Regina said.

I couldn't tell if she was kidding or not. "I'll have the oatmeal, then."

"Is that it?" she asked me incredulously.

"For now."

After she was gone, I asked my brother, "Are you sure we shouldn't be sitting at the bar near the register where everything's happening?"

"Annie, I know it goes against your nature to stay out of the fray, but we can't just dive in and start asking questions about Della and Cheryl."

"Why not?" I asked him.

"Why not indeed?" a man sitting solo in the booth beside us asked as he left his place and joined us without being asked. He was wearing a flannel shirt and faded blue jeans, so his uniform matched most of the men present, and a few of the ladies as well. He carried his coffee mug with him, and as he slid in beside my brother, he put it down on the table. "What brings you two to town?"

"We're here visiting family," I said.

"Oh, really? Anybody I know?"

Pat raised an eyebrow. "How could we possibly have any idea of everybody that you know?"

The stranger chuckled. "That's a point. Why don't you try me and we'll see?"

"Della Mahoney," I said.

There was a slight hitch to his smile before he answered, "I know Della."

"Did you know Cheryl Simmons as well?" I asked him.

A cloud covered his face for a moment. "That's a real shame, what happened to her. Did you two know her through Della?"

"We never met her," Pat said. That was my brother, honest to the point of it being a character flaw. "Has there been any more news about what happened?"

The stranger leaned forward as he whispered, "Don't quote me, but I heard she got conked on the noggin, rolled into the water unconscious, and drowned. I don't know how they can tell these things for sure, but evidently they can."

"If there's water in her lungs, then she had to have breathed in," I said. "If not, she was dead before she hit the lake."

"Are you two some kind of detectives or something?" he asked me.

"We read a lot of books and we watch a lot of television, too," Pat said, no doubt trying to keep our real purpose secret for a little while longer.

"Ghastly stuff, that. I'll take an old-fashioned western any day."

"Book or movie?" Pat asked him. My brother had also been known to watch or read an oater on more than one occasion. What was it about the romance of the old west that appealed to so many men? Given the choice, I'll take the miracles of modern drugs and air conditioning ten out of ten times myself.

"Both," he admitted.

Before they could start discussing their favorite westerns, I decided to try to keep the conversation from being derailed. "Why would anyone want to kill Cheryl Simmons?"

"That's a fair question," the man said. "She was wearing Della's hat, from what I heard."

"It was her jacket," I blurted out before being able to stop myself. I wasn't sure if we should have kept that fact a secret, but it was too late for that now.

"That makes more sense than just a hat," the man said and then took a large sip of coffee. "From the back, and in the dark to boot, I doubt anyone would be able to tell Cheryl from Della, and I've known them both for years. Do you two think that attack was made for your cousin?"

"Actually, she's our aunt," I said. "We're twins."

"The three of you?" he asked incredulously.

"No, just me and my brother," I said. Had he not just heard the "aunt" designation?

He studied us both for a moment before replying. "No offense, but you don't look anything alike to me."

"We're fraternal, not identical. That means that we were in the same womb at the same time, but in different eggs," Pat explained.

"Speaking of eggs, here yours come. Would you like me to leave so you can have some peace and quiet while you eat?"

"No, please stay," I said. We might be able to get some information out of this stranger, and I hated to pass up the chance.

After Regina delivered our orders, she asked, "You need anything, Gary?"

"No, I'm good," he said.

My spoon hovered over my oatmeal. "Are you Gary White, by any chance?"

He looked surprised by my identification. "How could you possibly know that? I know for a fact that I didn't introduce myself when I joined you."

"You made it a point not to, didn't you?" Pat asked him. "Could that have anything to do with the threats you made against our aunt a few days ago?"

"Hang on there, partner. I didn't make any threats toward anyone. Did Della say that I did?"

"She told us that you were so upset about the parade bypassing your hardware store that you threatened to burn it all down. Is that true, or are you calling her a liar?" I asked.

"Slow down. We had words, and I can't recall exactly what I said to her, but Della said much worse to me, and you can believe that whether you want to or not." He took a slow sip of coffee, and then he put his mug back on the table before he spoke again. "Your aunt thinks that whoever killed Cheryl was gunning for her, doesn't she?"

"Why do you say that?" I asked him, not wanting to give anything more away than I already had.

"It just makes sense. She's been acting odd all week. At first I thought it was because of the festival, but that's not the case, is it? So, she thinks she's got a target on her back, does she? No wonder she hasn't been herself lately."

"Her suspicions aren't entirely without merit," I told him.

"Has somebody actually taken a run at her?" Gary asked, lowering his voice as he did so. "That's not good."

"You're telling us," Pat said. "She's our family. How do you think we feel about it?"

"If there's anything I can do to help, and I mean anything, all you have to do is ask. I feel bad now for the hard words between us, and I aim to make things right," he said as he dug out his wallet. I was about to refuse his offer to buy us breakfast when he slipped a business card from his wallet and slid it across the table to me. "My home number's on that thing, so call me day or night if you need me."

"Why are you being so helpful to us?" Pat asked him. It was a worthy question that I was wondering about myself.

"You said it yourself. Knowing Della, half the town is going to believe that I had something to do with Cheryl's murder. Your aunt isn't afraid of sharing her thoughts with the rest of this sleepy little place, and before you know it, folks will be driving somewhere else for their hardware needs. Call my offer a healthy dose of self-interest, if that makes you feel any better."

"I can accept that," Pat said.

Gary made a motion to leave, but before he could go, I reached across the table and touched his arm lightly. "Are you sincere about your offer to help us?"

"Yes, ma'am. I wouldn't have made it if I hadn't been."

"Then stay right here and tell us about some of your fellow townsfolk."

He shrugged. "Who do you want to know about?"

"Let's start with Police Chief Cameron," Pat said.

"Who else have you got?" Gary asked, clearly uncomfortable talking about the chief of police.

"I thought you were going to help us?" I asked him.

"Cam isn't all that fond of your aunt. They went out for a while a long time ago, and from what I heard, he asked her out again a few days ago. She laughed at him, and that's likely to leave scorch marks on a man's heart, if you know what I mean."

So, at least that much of Aunt Della's story was true. "What about your mayor?"

"Davis? Did she say that he was sweet on her, too?" Gary asked me.

"She hinted as much," I said.

"Well, if he is, she'd better watch her back. Serena Jefferson laid her claim on that man a long time ago, and she wouldn't take well to trespassers."

So, Aunt Della wasn't nearly as delusional as Pat and I had first suspected.

"I don't get it. What's her charm?" my brother asked him candidly.

"It's simple, really. When your aunt talks to a man, she gives him her full attention. It's as though there's not another soul in the world, and nothing is more important than what you've got to say. It can be intoxicating at times."

"Have you ever had a thing for her yourself?" I asked him.

"Me? No. No ma'am. That's never going to happen."

Pat grinned. "You don't seem to be very sure of your answer."

"Don't get me wrong, Della is a fine woman, and a great listener, but I've had my heart broken too many times. I'm afraid if I fall in love again and it ends badly, it will be more than I can take. That's how my daddy died, and I don't want to follow in his footsteps."

"He died of a broken heart?" I asked, knowing that it didn't have anything to do with our case, but I wanted to know nonetheless. "Did your mother leave him?"

"In a way. The cancer got her. I thought it was going to kill him when she passed away, but to my surprise, he found himself another wife. Only she had more problems than anyone could have suspected. Six weeks into the marriage, she left with everything in their joint bank account. There was a note that said she was sorry that it didn't work out, and for the next six months, I watched my father slowly die right in front of me. He just gave up, you know?" There were tears in the corner of Gary's eyes, and without realizing what I was doing, I reached out and patted his hand gently.

"I'm so sorry," I said.

"It's all ancient history now," the hardware store owner said. He shook his head once, wiped away the tears with the back of his hand, and then he stood, throwing a twenty on the table. "Breakfast is on me, folks. Happy hunting."

Before we could protest, he was gone.

"What do you make of that?" Pat asked me.

"It's just about the saddest story I've heard," I told him.

"I'm not talking about his dad's broken heart. Gary managed to confirm everything that Della told us, with one glaring exception."

"What's that?" I asked, still thinking about the tragic story of his father.

"Della claimed that she and Gary had a real argument, but he seemed to downplay it, didn't he? I wonder if anyone overheard them arguing?"

"We can always ask around," I said as Regina came up, scowling at us both.

"You two Della's kin?" she asked harshly.

"We are," Pat said.

I kept waiting for Regina to say something, but after a moment, she just shook her head and walked away.

"What was that all about?" I asked my brother.

"I don't know, but I've got a feeling that she's not a fan."

"Maybe she wants the mayor for herself, too," I said with a smile.

"Maybe," he answered.

After our breakfast was over, Pat grabbed the twenty, as well as our bill, and we walked to the register together. "You're not going to actually let Gary pay for our meal, are you?"

"Why not?" Pat asked as he handed Regina the twenty Gary had left behind.

I waited until we were outside on the curb before I asked, "Care to explain what just happened?"

"Don't worry, I was just teasing. I used his twenty, but I'm planning on paying him back the next time we see him," he replied.

"When are we going to do that?"

"As soon as we speak with our other suspects. Maybe if we get lucky, we'll find someone who overheard that exchange between Della and him. In the meantime, we've got other folks we need to speak with first."

"Where should we start?" I asked him.

"Town hall sounds good to me, since two of our suspects work there. Should we question them separately or stick together?"

"Together," I said without hesitation. "Always together."

CHAPTER 9: PAT

"**I**S THE MAYOR IN?" I asked the pretty young brunette behind the desk in city hall as I gave her my brightest smile.

"He is," she said, though it was clear that my charm had no effect on her. "Did you have an appointment?"

"No, but we were hoping that he could fit us in. We just met him last night."

"You're Della's people, aren't you?" she asked with a smile. If there was any animosity between them, I couldn't see it. Perhaps this was one of the times where our aunt's sense of dramatics came into play.

"We are," I said as I extended a hand. "I'm Pat Marsh, and this is my twin sister, Annie."

She took my hand and then Annie's. "I've always been fascinated by twins. They run in my family."

"Are you one yourself?" Annie asked her.

"I wish. It must be so cool."

"It can be," I said with a grin.

"More so for him than me, most times," she added.

"I bet. Let me see if Davis has a second for you."

She stood and walked from behind her desk into the mayor's office. Once she was gone, Annie said, "She's cute enough to get someone her own age. Davis has to be somewhere around thirty years older than she is."

"Maybe she finds older men attractive," I said.

"Then you wouldn't qualify," she answered with a smile. "You're not old enough."

"I've got someone in my life, remember?"

"I know that. I just want to make sure that you do. Jenna is the best thing that's happened to you in a long time." I knew she was referring to Molly Fennel, my former love, and she was right. Molly and I had too much of a history to ever put the past completely behind us, but I was with Jenna now, and I was happy about it.

"No worries on that count. I'm not about to mess that up," I said.

"Good."

Serena came back and stood in the open doorway. "He's got some time for you right now, but you need to make it quick." She turned and looked at her boss and scolded him. "Don't take over ten minutes, or I'll have to throw them out," she said good-naturedly. "You have a meeting with the planning commission, and you skipped out on the last one."

"I got distracted," he said with a grin.

"That's where I come in, to keep you on the straight and narrow."

As we stepped inside, I said, "We won't keep him long."

"I'm just having a little fun with him," Serena said. She closed the door behind us, and Davis stood until we were seated across from him. For the mayor, his desk was rather nondescript, and I wondered if it had first seen life in a high school classroom. The top was scarred from decades of hard use, but somehow it seemed to fit Davis just fine.

"She seems nice," Annie said.

"For a nag, she's okay," he answered with a grin. "Not that I don't need someone keeping me on schedule. Before I hired her, I missed half of the meetings I was supposed to be attending, and I like the way she teases me into action."

"Is there anything else going on between the two of you?" Annie asked lightly.

"What? Do you mean romantically? She's just a child! I'm thirty years older than she is, Annie."

"Still, it's been known to happen," my sister pushed a little harder.

"Not to me. I like women I can share a common history with."

"Does that mean you only go out with people that you've dated before?" I asked him.

"No, I mean general history. My cutoff line is the first moon landing."

"I don't follow," Annie said.

"If they were born before Neil Armstrong took that first step, then I'll date them. After that, and there's not as much to talk about as I would like."

It was an interesting approach, and I couldn't blame him for it. It would be hard enough for me to go out with someone ten years younger than I was, let alone thirty. I had a friend from school who kept marrying eighteen-year-old girls. He'd started in high school, getting Miranda Huggins pregnant our junior year and eloping to Las Vegas. When that didn't work out, he'd married Sarah Lawson eight years later, who also happened to be eighteen at the time. After Sarah left him, he started dating yet another eighteen-year-old, and I wondered if he'd ever be able to break the cycle.

"How about Serena? Did I see a twinkle in her eye when she looked at you?" Annie asked.

I had to hand it to my sister; she'd steered the conversation so elegantly that I wanted to applaud.

"Hardly. I'm more of a crazy uncle to her, as far as I can tell. The last I heard, she was dating someone long distance in Raleigh, but I try not to dig too deeply into her personal life." He paused a moment, and then the mayor/newspaperman leaned back in his chair. "I'm sure you didn't come by to discuss my love life. What can I do for you?"

"Have you had any luck discovering what they found at the crime scene last night?" I asked him. We had a valuable resource at our disposal, and I wasn't about to ignore it.

"Yes. It's most likely the murder weapon," he answered gravely.

"What was it?" I asked him.

"I probably shouldn't be telling you this, but it was a heavy-duty flashlight. Apparently Cheryl was struck from behind with something around the size of it, or shaped a lot like it. It didn't kill her, but it must have knocked her out the second it hit. The official cause of death is drowning, and the report lists foul play. She was deliberately murdered."

"Maybe not," I said. "They may have wanted to just knock her unconscious. You saw the slope of the path near where they found her body. She could have easily rolled into the water before her assailant could stop her progress."

"Doesn't matter. It's still homicide if it happened as a direct result of the assault," the mayor said. I had a feeling he'd looked that up upon learning about the blow to the head.

I remembered that Della had told us that she'd loaned just such a flashlight to Cheryl the night she was murdered. Was that true, or was our aunt covering her tracks for a crime she committed herself? It sounded outlandish at first, but what did we really know about the woman? Had she had her own reasons to want to see her best friend dead? If so, the supposed attempts on her life might help muddy the trail. Then again, it hadn't been my imagination last night; someone had tried to get into her house long after anyone should have been making the attempt. This was getting more confusing than it had first appeared. "Any idea who the flashlight belongs to?" I asked him.

Davis frowned upon hearing the question. "From what I've learned, there were no distinguishing characteristics on it, aside from the section that was a little dinged up from where it most likely hit Cheryl. Why, do you know something I don't?"

"I'm just asking questions, hoping to uncover something that's relevant," I said. It was the complete and utter truth, and yet it still managed quite nicely as a lie. I needed to have another talk with Della, but until I did, the mayor was just going to have to be satisfied with my obfuscation.

It made me proud when Annie didn't react at all to my statement, though I could tell from the look in her eye that she'd made the connection as well.

"Is there anything else you can tell us?" I asked him.

"Honestly, I've probably said more than I should have. How do you two manage to do that?"

"Do what?" Annie asked.

"Make it so easy to tell you things I shouldn't," he replied. After glancing at his watch, the mayor said, "I hate to keep bailing out on you, but Serena's right; I really can't miss another meeting."

As he started to stand, I said, "Just one more question."

"Fire away, but make it quick."

"Are you in love with our aunt?" I asked him.

It took him a few seconds to come up with an answer to a pretty straightforward question. "That's an odd question. What gave you that idea?"

"According to her, you've asked her out on more than one occasion, and now you're living in the house right beside her. It's a fair question."

"Della is an interesting woman; I'll give you that," the mayor replied. "I've expressed interest in dating her in the past, which she has politely declined. The fact that I bought that house has a great deal more to do with its location on the water than it does its proximity to your aunt. Now, if there's nothing else, I've really got to go."

We all walked out into the hallway together, and I was surprised to find Serena standing just beside the door. Had she been eavesdropping on our conversation the entire time?

She said quickly, "Good. I was just coming to get you. Here are the papers you need for your meeting."

Serena handed him a sheaf of paperwork, which he gratefully took. "What would I do without you?" he asked her with a grin.

"Fail miserably at whatever you attempted, most likely," she answered with a warm smile of her own.

After her boss disappeared, I heard Annie say, "He's really something, isn't he?"

"Davis is a good man, and he has the potential to be a great mayor. He just needs a little nudge every now and then."

"And that's where you come in, right?" Annie asked.

"I like to think I have a hand in it," she replied.

"It would be hard not to have feelings for a man with that much charisma, especially when you work so closely with him."

"Me and Davis? Hardly. He's old enough to be my father." She appeared suitably outraged by the notion, but I couldn't tell if she was sincere in her protests or not.

"But he's not related to you," I said. "Surely you've thought about it."

"No, I can honestly say that it's never crossed my mind. Besides, I have a boyfriend."

"A long-distance one, correct?" Annie asked.

"How did you know that?"

"Davis told us," my sister replied.

"Well, it's true enough." Her phone rang on her desk, but before she answered it, she turned to us and asked, "Is there anything else?"

"Just one thing," I said. "Did you know Cheryl Simmons very well?"

"We were aware of each other's presence enough to say hello if we met on the street or in the grocery store, but that's about the extent of it. Why?"

"Just curious," I said. "See you later."

"I have no doubt of it," she replied. "After all, Gateway Lake is a small town."

"That it is," I said as Annie and I left her office space.

"What was that all about?" my sister asked me once we were well away from the mayor's office.

"What do you mean?"

"We left before we could ask her for an alibi, and we never did get a chance to ask Davis for his, either."

"The time frame when the murder could have occurred is so spread out that alibis aren't going to do us a bit of good with this case," I told her. "Anyone in town could have done it, or in the state, for that matter. I thought about asking her some more pointed questions, but I didn't know how to phrase them without warning her that they were both suspects in the woman's homicide."

"Isn't that the exact premise we're working from, though?" Annie asked me. "*Somebody* killed that woman."

"Unless she dropped the flashlight, tripped on a root in the dark, and drowned, all by accident."

"If that's what happened," my sister said, "then we're not doing ourselves any good snooping around town. We have to work with the idea that someone was so obsessed with Aunt Della that they killed Cheryl Simmons by mistake."

"Did Serena seem obsessed to you? How about Davis?" I asked my sister.

"No, not particularly. Then again, their behaviors could have both been covering up their true feelings toward our aunt."

I shook my head. "I have a hard time believing that after speaking with both of them. Isn't it possible that Della's imagination has gotten the better of her this time? Davis didn't seem to be in love with her, and Serena didn't seem all that jealous, either."

"Are you saying that Aunt Della read both people wrong?" Annie asked me.

"I'm just saying that they both seemed perfectly rational in their reactions to her," I answered.

"Davis never answered our question, though. Did you notice that?"

"What are you talking about?" I asked her.

"We asked him if he was in love with Aunt Della, and he never answered."

"Are you sure about that?" I thought back to the conversation and realized that Annie was right. Davis had managed to avoid answering our question altogether by diverting the conversation from it. "You're right. I missed that. Is it significant? After all, he could have just lied to us."

"I think he's too good a politician not to leave himself a way out if we find out the truth later."

"How about his feelings for Serena?"

73

"I think he really does think of her as a quirky niece, but how Serena feels is a different matter altogether."

I was surprised by my sister's observation, since the secretary had struck me as being open and sincere. "She smiled when she heard Della's name, and she couldn't have been nicer to the two of us if she'd tried."

"I don't know. It didn't feel right to me, for some reason," Annie said. "I don't completely trust her."

"Even though we don't have any reason not to?" I asked her.

"Aunt Della considers her a threat," Annie answered. "That's enough for me."

"Even after our conversation?"

"Even then."

There was no use discussing it further until we had more information. "Where should we go now?" I asked her.

"We could always go speak with Gary again," she suggested.

"Until we have more information, I'd like to delay that for a little while. I have another idea, but I have a feeling that you're not going to like it."

"Try me," Annie asked.

"Let's talk to our aunt again," I said.

"To call her a liar about what she told us before?" Annie asked me, being more than a little bit defensive.

"No, but we need to know if she has any solid proof that Davis is willing to kill her if he can't have her all to himself and that Serena wants to see her dead so she doesn't lose the man of her dreams. Some of Della's stories I can buy, but some of them just don't add up, especially after we've spoken with the parties involved."

"Okay, we can certainly ask her for some clarification," Annie conceded, "but we can't browbeat her, Pat. She may not be your favorite person in the world, but she's family, and she deserves better than that."

"Annie, when I have ever browbeat anyone?" I asked her calmly.

"I just know how you feel."

"I'm trying to warm up to her, but that doesn't mean she gets a free pass. We need to push her just as hard as we would anyone else we didn't happen to be related to. It might get a little tense, but we still need to do it. If you can't go along with that, then I'll give you a free pass. You can make your excuses and go do something else, but she and I are having that talk, whether you like it or not. I'm sorry to go against your wishes, but it's how it has to be."

"If your gut is telling you that, then I'll have your back," Annie answered quietly. "You know that."

"Even against Della?" I asked.

"Even against Kathleen," she replied. It was the only answer I would accept from her. It had been the two of us against the world since our births, and I hoped that it would end that way in the end, but not until we were both old and gray, a pair of ancient, cranky geezers.

"Thank you. Now, let's go see if Della can clear things up for us any."

CHAPTER 10: ANNIE

I WASN'T ALL THAT THRILLED WITH the prospect of asking our aunt such hard questions about the things she'd recently told us, but I knew in my heart that Pat was right. We couldn't let Aunt Della off the hook just because we were family. What we had to ask her might alienate her from us again, but it was a risk that we had to take. I was steeling myself for the confrontation when I was surprised to see someone leaving Della's house as we arrived.

I was getting ready to introduce myself when the older, rail-thin woman turned and found us approaching. She frowned for a second, and then sunlight appeared on her face. "Annie! Patrick! I'm so glad to finally get to meet you!"

She was certainly enthusiastic. "It's good to meet you, too," I said. "And you are?"

She blushed a little. "I'm Henrietta Long. Your aunt and I have been great friends forever."

"You ran the Winter Wonderland together," Pat said. "She's told us about you, too."

"Only good things, I hope," she said with a giggle, though she was clearly older than Della. It sounded odd coming from her.

"What brings you by the house?" I asked her.

"We were going to settle up all of the accounts from the fundraiser, but silly me, I left the ledger books at home. None of those fancy computers for me! Given your visit, we've decided to wait until tomorrow to go over the final numbers. Are you staying long? She'd really love it if you could. I know it's probably a huge imposition, but it would mean so much to her."

Wow, this woman was good. We'd only just met her, and here she was making us feel guilty for planning such a short stay with our aunt. I had to laugh. "We'll stay as long as we can, but we have a business to run."

"She's told me all about the Iron. It sounds delightful. I'd love to see it someday."

I didn't see how that was possible, given the fact that our aunt had never stepped foot in the place, but I was willing to go along with the ruse just to get this woman gone. "We like it," I said. "Sorry to cut this short, but we really need to talk to our aunt now."

"Of course. I was just on my way. Have a wonderful day."

"You, too," Pat said, shaking his head a little as he did. After Henrietta was gone, he looked at me and rolled his eyes, something that never ceased to make me laugh. I knew my brother's opinion of the woman without him having to say a word.

Della was surprised to find us back so soon. "That was fast."

"We need to ask you a few things," Pat said gravely.

"That sounds serious. What have you heard?"

He didn't answer her question, and neither did I as I asked her a question of my own. "Della, do you honestly believe that Davis is in love with you?"

"It's clear by the way he looks at me, and the man's certainly asked me out enough times! Why, did he deny that?"

"No, he made it perfectly clear that he asked you, but he said that when you weren't interested, he dropped it."

It was clearly a blow to her ego to believe that any man couldn't fall helplessly in love with her, and then just cast her aside. "You said yourself that he might have done that just to be near me."

"And you explained that it was more to get a house by the lake than to be close by," I reminded her. This line of questioning had been my brother's idea, but that didn't mean that I wasn't going to embrace it.

"Is that what he told you? Well, he had more on his mind than just a view. The more I think about it, the more I realize that you are right. He did it to get closer to me."

"Also, we met Serena Jefferson while we were in city hall," Pat said. "She seems nice, and she smiled brightly when she found out that we were related. She seemed to genuinely like you."

Della frowned for a moment before she replied. "Of course she'd present that front to you, but I know the truth."

It was pretty clear that we weren't going to be able to shake our aunt's beliefs.

Pat must have thought so, too, because his next question took us in a completely different direction. "Cheryl was most likely killed because of a flashlight that matches the description of the one you said you gave her the night she was murdered."

"What? Are you sure? I thought they found her in the water. What did my flashlight have to do with that?" The new information seemed to rock her back onto her heels.

"It's true that she drowned, but the flashlight blow to the back of the head is what sent her into the water, unconscious," Pat said.

"Why are you telling me this?" she asked, the fright in her voice obvious as her gaze darted from my brother to me. "Do you honestly think that I killed my best friend? Why would I do that?"

"We don't know," Pat said, "but hard questions have to be asked."

"By you? But we're family!" She was near a breakdown. I could see it in her eyes and hear it in her voice.

"We are. That's why we're asking you point blank," I said calmly. "I'm going to ask you this one time, and then we'll drop it forever. Aunt Della, did you have anything to do with what happened to Cheryl Simmons?"

"I did not. I swear it on your mother's grave."

I could have done without that particular pledge, but I believed her. She might have been deluding herself about the mayor's intentions and his secretary's jealousy, but she hadn't killed her friend. I glanced at Pat, who nodded in agreement when we made eye contact. Della might be a bit of a drama queen, but neither one of us thought that she was a cold-blooded killer.

"Fine. We believe you," I said. "Let's just assume for the moment that Davis and Serena are in the clear. Where does that leave us?"

"With just one person, as far as I'm concerned," Della said.

"The town's chief of police," Pat said flatly, clearly unsure of her assessment.

"Most policemen are good people," Della said, "but it's no guarantee that all of them are. Cam could have done it if he thought it was me on that path and not Cheryl."

"I don't know," Pat said. "It seems a little farfetched to me."

"So is murder being committed in our sleepy little town, but it happened nonetheless," Della said. "If I were you, I'd focus on Cam, but don't forget about Davis and Serena completely. I know they can both put up convincing fronts, but don't let them fool you. Davis is a politician at heart, and lying comes easily to him. As for Serena, she's fooled better people than you two in the past, but she's not duping me." Della took a deep breath, and then she continued, "I understand you feeling the need to challenge me, but I didn't kill my friend, and I'm not losing my mind. Someone is trying to kill me, and if you two don't do something about it, the next time they are going to succeed. If you waste your time trying to prove that I'm either culpable or downright delusional, than you might as well not be here, because I'm already a dead woman."

"We're not going to let that happen," I said, though I had no idea how I was going to keep that particular promise. "Right, Pat?"

"Not if we can help it," he amended.

Our assurances seemed to give her some comfort. "That's all that I can ask. Maybe we should call your sister and see what she thinks," Della suggested.

"We're doing fine on our own," I said. "Kathleen has her own problems, and it wouldn't be fair to drag her into this. Pat and I are perfectly capable of solving this."

"I sincerely hope so," Della said. "Are you hungry, by any chance?"

"We just ate breakfast a few hours ago," I said.

"Of course you did. Why don't you come back at noon? I'll have a meal ready for you then."

"You don't have to cook for us, Aunt Della," I said.

"I understand that, but then again, you both didn't have to drop everything and come to my aid, either. Let me do this for you."

"Fine," I said.

Pat nodded his agreement.

"In the meantime, we have more work to do before then."

"I know I can count on you," she said as we left the house once again.

I looked at Pat once we were outside again. "What do you think?"

"She's either telling us the truth, or she's deluded herself into believing that it's all true. I have a feeling that both things might be accurate."

"What do you mean?"

"What if she honestly believes that Davis is in love with her and that Serena is wickedly jealous of the fact, but neither thing is true? I don't doubt for a second that she believes every bit of it, but whether that makes it so or not, I have no idea, and there's no one we can ask."

"There's always Chief Cameron," I said.

Pat shook his head. "I doubt he's in the mood to share much with us at the moment. We have another source in town, though."

"Gary White," I said.

Pat shrugged. "Maybe he knows something, and after all, he offered to help us at breakfast."

"Why not?" I asked. "What do we have to lose?"

"The list is too long to even discuss," Pat replied. As he looked back at Della's house, he said, "If we hadn't had our late-night visitor, I would be less inclined to believe her about anything, but *someone* was trying to get in last night."

"That could mean that they're afraid of something," I said.

"Sure, but what? Why is Della such a threat to someone?"

"That's what we need to find out."

———— ⊷◉◈◉⊶ ————

I could see my brother's eyes light up the moment we walked into Gary White's hardware store. To me, it looked as though we'd stepped through some kind of magic portal back in time. There were trays and shelves holding nothing but nuts, bolts, washers, and metal things that I couldn't even begin to identify. Though the weather outside was still frigid, packets of garden seeds were displayed prominently at the front of the store, along with loose seeds stored in wooden sections that were parceled out with aluminum scoops. There were kerosene heater wicks, snow sleds and shovels, and bibbed overalls that hung from the rafters like empty scarecrow starter kits. The floors were stained from years of abuse, gouges filled in darkly and even gaps in the wood where dust must have drifted down to the basement in dirty snowfalls. I was about to say something when I spotted a section that instantly caught my eye.

Gary had cast iron cookware for sale, and not the new, freshly minted stuff that still sported its factory seasoning. This was cast iron from another generation, when the metal was poured thin and true, and the quality couldn't be touched today. I picked up a Griswold #6 fry pan and marveled that underneath a fine layer of dust, there was a truly magnificent piece of art. There was a tag dangling from the opening in the handle that was hard to read, but as I wiped the dirt from it, I saw that it was for sale for $14.99. Beside it was a cast iron Dutch oven, also an ancient Griswold, and priced at $24.99. Without saying a word to my brother, I took both pieces and walked straight to the register.

"I'd like to buy these, please," I said.

"What about talking to Gary first?" Pat asked me.

"He can wait," I said as I showed him the prices.

I was glad that my brother didn't play poker, because his eyes lit up like Christmas trees when he saw what I'd found, and at what price. I handed the man three twenties, more than enough to cover the purchase price and sales tax, just as Gary approached.

"Doing a little shopping, Annie?" he asked.

"A little," I said, reaching my hand out for my change and, more importantly, the receipt. Once the transaction was complete, there would be no take-backs, if Gary even realized the bargain I'd just gotten.

The clerk was in the process of handing me my change and the coveted receipt when Gary put a hand on his employee's and stopped it before it could reach me. "Hang on a second."

"I'm paying your asking price," I said. "What's the problem?"

He ignored me and lifted up what I considered my skillet. When he saw the price on it, he called loudly to the back, "Tommy, come up here, please."

"I'm helping Mrs. Wilkins right now," a voice called back.

"Now," Gary said, and it was clear that he wasn't messing around.

"Is there a problem?" Pat asked him, but the store owner just held up a hand, demanding that we wait.

A young man in his early twenties came up to the front, looking confused as to why he was being summoned so urgently, but the moment his gaze saw what his boss was holding, he started stammering. "I forgot. I'm sorry. I was going to do it yesterday, but I got distracted."

Gary turned to me. "Young Thomas was supposed to pull these from inventory yesterday. I have a buyer online that is willing to pay considerably more than the asking price for these two pieces."

"I'm sorry about that," I said, "but your cashier rang up the sale and took my money. The transaction is complete as far as I'm concerned."

"Do you have a receipt?" he asked me, knowing full well that it was still in his cashier's hand.

"No, but I have witnesses," I said. I wouldn't have minded paying more for those pieces, but I didn't feel as though I should. After all, he ran the store, he priced his inventory, and it wasn't fair to jack up the price after an offer and acceptance had been made. I wasn't sure if what he was trying to do was legal or not, but I knew full well that it wasn't ethical, at least as far as I was concerned.

Gary considered it another moment, and then he forced a smile. "You're perfectly right. Enjoy your new purchases in good health."

"Thanks. I will," I said as I took the receipt and my change and handed the cookery to Pat.

"I'm really sorry, Mr. White. I won't let it happen again," Tommy said, clearly relieved that the issue had been resolved.

"I know you won't, because you're fired," Gary said.

"Hang on a second," I interrupted. "I don't want them that badly. You can have the cookware back if you return my money. Just don't fire him."

Gary pointed to a sign above the register. It said, in old-fashioned script, NO EXCHANGES, NO RETURNS. ALL SALES ARE FINAL. "Sorry, it's out of my hands."

"I said that I was sorry, Mr. White," Tommy pled.

"What? Sorry. I didn't realize that you were still here," the store owner said in an icy voice. Tommy looked as though he'd just been electrocuted as he stumbled out the door.

"I didn't mean for that to happen," I stammered. The great deal that I'd just gotten wasn't so great anymore, and what was worse, there was nothing I could do to make things right again.

"That young man needs to learn that there are consequences in this life for every action we take," Gary said as he shook his head. "It's a lesson that all of us should remember." He straightened a few things on the counter, and then he turned back to us. "Was there something else I could help you with today?"

"We were wondering if your offer to help us was still open," Pat said. I had to hand it to my brother; I hadn't had the guts to suggest that, not after what had just happened.

"Sorry, but I'm a little busy at the moment. It appears that I have to find a new employee." He nodded once, and then he walked back to the back where his office was located, at least according to the sign that hung from the rafters.

"Did I really just get that kid fired?" I asked out loud.

It had been more of a rhetorical question in my mind, but the cashier answered it anyway. "Don't feel too bad about it. He's been itching to fire Tommy for weeks. This just gave him the opportunity to do it and blame someone else."

"Will he be okay?" I asked.

"No worries there. Tommy will land on his feet. He hated this job anyway."

"Because of his boss?" Pat asked him softly.

"No. That couldn't be it," the young man said as he nodded slightly in disagreement with what he'd just said. "Everyone loves working here."

"Jason, I need you for a moment," Gary called out from the back.

"I hope we didn't get you into trouble, too," I said softly as he started to go.

"He's not going to fire me, at least not until he can replace Tommy. If he did, that would mean that he'd have to pitch in himself and make Tillie actually work too, and none of that's going to happen, you can trust me on that. She's too young, and way too pretty to soil her pretty little hands," he said softly with a grin.

"Now, Jason!"

"Have a nice day," the clerk said as he winked at us and turned to face his boss.

———

Once we were on the sidewalk, Pat asked, "Well, Annie, was it worth it?"

"Of course not. I didn't mean to get that young man fired, and you know it."

"That's not what I'm talking about," Pat said doggedly. "Gary offered to act as a source for us, but that's gone forever now."

"Pat, they are Griswolds," I said, as if that were enough. It should have been, given our love of all things cast iron.

"I know," my brother relented. "You didn't do anything wrong. You even tried to rescind the sale, but he wasn't about to allow that, was he?"

"He's a bully, and I don't like him, no matter how good a first impression he made on me at the diner this morning," I said.

"Agreed. I was wondering before about Della's story about the two of them fighting, but I can surely see it now. Gary White seems perfectly capable of trying to kill someone who thwarts him, and from what we've heard, Della did that and more."

"So his name stays on our list," I said. "I suppose it wasn't a complete failure."

"No, and we got some spiffy new cast iron to boot."

We started walking back to Della's house when I spotted the young man I'd just gotten fired. He was sitting on a bench two blocks from the hardware store, staring off into space. I handed the pan I'd been carrying to my brother, who added it to the Dutch oven he was already hauling, and took a deep breath. "I'm so sorry that just happened," I said as I walked up to him.

"You know what? You did me a favor," Tommy said, trying his best to muster a grin. "I've been dying to get up the nerve to quit, and now that it's out of my hands, I'm ready to start living."

"What will you do?"

"Whatever I want to," he said with a grin. "That is one wicked man there. I'd watch my step around him if I were you. He's all smiles to the customers, but the folks who work for him see the real man underneath. He's not one to cross."

"Is he capable of murder?" I asked.

Tommy shrugged. "That, and more probably."

I didn't want to know what "more" might entail. "May I pay you something for the trouble I've caused you, no matter how inadvertent it might have been?" I pushed a fresh twenty and the change I'd gotten back toward him, which was all of the money that I had on me.

He shook his head, and as he stood and started to walk away, he turned to say, "I appreciate the offer, but I'm good. Have a great day."

"You, too," I said, and then I turned back to my brother. "Any ideas about what we should do next, now that I've blown our only confidante left in town?"

"We need to get this stuff back to Della's," Pat said. "I'm not going to walk all over town lugging it all around, but you're more than welcome to if you'd like."

I took the skillet back from him, leaving him with the heavier Dutch oven, but at least it had a wire handle he could use. Still, the cookware was heavy, as it should have been.

"No, I think that's a great idea."

CHAPTER 11: PAT

"**M**AYBE WE SHOULD HAVE DRIVEN when we left the house," I said to Annie as I lugged the new, at least new to us, cast iron Dutch oven. The thing was getting heavier with every step I took. I'd replayed what had happened back at the hardware store in my mind, and I couldn't see how what had happened to Tommy had been my sister's fault, but I still knew that she felt horrible about it. We both loved good deals, but not at someone else's expense.

"I can go get the car if you want to sit at the curb here and wait for me," Annie said with the hint of a smile.

"No, I think I can tough it out," I said.

We were two blocks from Della's place when a car suddenly rushed toward us from behind. I was glad there was a sidewalk, because the maniac was flying. Then I saw that it was Chief Cameron driving one of the town's squad cars, and I almost found myself wishing for a maniac instead.

He pulled the car up and slammed on the brakes right in front of us. Flipping on his lights almost as an afterthought, he got out of the cruiser and walked over to us.

"What exactly do you two think you're doing?" he asked heatedly as he confronted us on the walkway.

"We're walking back to our aunt's place," I said. "Why, is there a law against using the sidewalk, or did we just make an illegal purchase of cast iron cookware?"

"You know what I'm talking about. You're digging into Cheryl Simmons's murder."

"Actually, we're not," Annie said calmly.

"That's not what I heard," the chief hesitantly replied.

"Well, I can't comment on your sources and their reliability unless you give me some names," Annie said calmly.

It just made the police chief angrier. "I'm not about to tell you that."

"Then we can't help you," I said, matching my twin sister's tone. "If that's all you wanted, are we free to go?"

"Do you promise me that you're not going around town asking questions about what happened to Cheryl Simmons?" he asked us.

"Oh, we're doing some of that all right," I said.

He looked at me in disbelief at first. "Why?"

Without thinking, I told him, "Someone's trying to kill our aunt, and we're not going to just stand by and watch it happen." I suddenly realized that we'd meant to keep that confidential, and now I'd just blurted it out in the middle of town. I couldn't help myself, though, and when I glanced at my sister, she nodded her approval. That was all I needed, so I quickly recounted the list of Della's suspicions.

Chief Cameron appeared to take it all in, and then, in an incredulous voice, he asked us, "Do you really believe that she's telling the truth?"

"Why wouldn't we? I'd think the murder would just reinforce her story," Annie said.

"For the last time, Cheryl wasn't killed because she was wearing Della's coat," he said with a look of disgust on his face.

"You're entitled to your theory, and we're entitled to ours," I said.

"As a matter of fact, that's not true at all. I'm the police chief, and you run a hardware store in another town."

"Actually, it's more of a general store/grill/post office," I corrected him.

"I don't care if you sell socks for a living," he shouted. Getting himself a little more under control, he added, "You have no right to be doing what you're doing."

"The last time I checked, we were free to walk on the sidewalk, buy cast iron products, and talk to people about something that concerns us, and you can't stop us from doing any of it," I said firmly.

"I can lock you up," he growled.

"You can try," I said, " but we both know we'll be out before the ink's dry on the paperwork. Do you really want to open yourself up to a lawsuit like that?" I was bluffing, but I hoped that he couldn't see that. I remained stony, and so did my sister.

When the police chief saw that we weren't going to allow him to scare us off, he said, "I can't guarantee your safety if you keep digging around in this."

"I didn't think Della had anyone after her," I said. "If what you say is correct, why would we be in any danger?"

"And why would you threaten us like that if we weren't on to something?" Annie added.

"I never threatened you," he said.

"My mistake. It sure sounded like a threat to me. How about you, Pat?"

I shrugged. "I'm with you. I definitely felt threatened just then."

"You two think you're funny, don't you?" Chief Cameron asked us.

"We have our moments," I conceded.

"Maybe, but this isn't one of them. You've been warned."

"Got it. Threatened and warned. You've covered them both." I looked at him for another moment before I asked, "Is there anything else?"

He didn't answer. Instead, the police chief just shook his head and got back into his car.

As he sped off, Annie looked at me and grinned. "Somebody's not happy with our investigation, are they?"

"No, the police chief seemed to be a bit miffed with us," I answered.

"I'm not talking about that. He was just trying to carry out someone else's wishes. Think about it. How could he know that we've been going around town asking questions if someone didn't complain about it to him? We've got someone on edge, so I have a hunch that we must be getting warmer."

"I didn't think of it that way," I admitted.

"That's why there are two of us. After all, two heads are better than one."

"Unless they just have one hat to share between them," I said with a grin. Maybe it wasn't that funny, but I felt as though the tension of the moment needed a little relief.

"Why don't you let me carry the Dutch oven for a while?" Annie asked as she reached for the handle.

I didn't give it up, though. "If you do that, then what will I have to complain about?"

She smiled at me as she lowered her hand. "I'm sure you'd think of something, but let's not tax that tiny little brain of yours, okay?"

"It's the same size as yours," I said.

"Perhaps, but I use mine a lot more efficiently than you do."

I decided not to challenge her assertion. I needed to save my breath for the rest of our hike. After we'd walked a little ways, I asked my sister, "So, who do you think we rattled with our questioning? Did Gary White call him?"

"He doesn't seem the type to cry for help, does he?"

"Well, I'm pretty sure that Davis wouldn't run to him," I said.

"Serena might, depending on how close they are. I'm honestly not sure. Who else did we talk to today about Della's suspicions?"

"Nobody that I can think of," I said. I glanced at my watch and realized that quite a bit of time had passed since we'd left Della's the last time. "Would you look at that? It's almost lunchtime."

Annie glanced at hers as well. "Not for another half an hour."

"Tell that to my stomach. I didn't get to finish my breakfast."

"Fine," she said. "When we get back to Aunt Della's, we can drop this stuff off, grab a quick bite, and then start back up this afternoon. I don't know what she's making, but surely there will be something worth eating."

"Start back up and do what, actually? I was under the impression that we'd already spoken to our suspects once, and without new information, what good will it do us to interview them again?"

"I don't know. We clearly need to think of a new game plan. There must be something we can do," Annie said.

"If there is, I don't know what it might be."

She frowned in thought for a minute before she suggested, "Why don't we eat, and then we'll talk about it again? Maybe our subconscious minds will be able to come up with something if we don't think about anything for a while."

I smiled at her. "You know me. Not thinking is one of my favorite things to do."

I'd set her up with a softball pitch, and she hit it over the wall. "You don't have to tell me that. I work with you every day, remember?"

I laughed, and we finally made it back to Della's house with our newfound objects safely. No one had offered us a ride along the way, but my twin sister and I had elicited a few stares as we'd walked carrying our cast iron purchases. It amazed me how many folks would rather peek out behind their blinds than just come out onto their front porches to get a better look at us. It felt to me as though the closer we got to our aunt's house, the more stares we generated.

Without even meaning to, it appeared that my sister and I were generating quite a bit of interest in Gateway Lake just by our presence.

I wasn't all that excited about getting that much attention, but then again, maybe if the attempted killer knew that we were out there searching for them, they'd give up their mission to murder our aunt.

I doubted it, though.

Whoever was doing it seemed quite determined to carry out their original quest, whether we were involved or not.

I started to knock on the front door when Annie laughed at me and grabbed the handle instead. "We don't need to knock, Pat," she said.

"Maybe you don't," I replied as I followed her inside. I wasn't sure

I felt good about just barging in. Despite my earlier warnings, the front door had been unlocked. I needed to speak to her about that, but not just yet. The place smelled amazing, and I followed my nose, and my sister, into the kitchen. When I walked into the room, I saw that the small dining room table just off the kitchen was covered in dishes, from entrees to sides to desserts. "Are we interrupting something? It looks as though you're having a party. We can always go back to Moe's for lunch," I volunteered, though in truth everything looked and smelled wonderful.

"Silly, this is for the two of you," she said. "Do you see anything you like?"

"It *all* looks wonderful," Annie said as she put her cast iron skillet down on one of the few free spaces on the kitchen counter. "You shouldn't have gone to so much trouble."

"Of course I should have." She grinned at the bounty and added with a smile, "I clearly couldn't decide what to make."

"So you made everything," I said with a grin of my own, putting my Dutch oven down on the floor out of the way.

"Is it too much?"

"Not if you don't mind having leftovers for the next few weeks," I said.

Annie nudged me a little as she said, "It's perfect. Thank you."

"I had fun cooking for you," she said, and then she glanced at the new pieces we'd just brought in. "Did you bring some cast iron with you from home?"

"No, we bought a few Griswold pieces at the hardware store in town," Annie said.

"Griswold? What's that mean?"

"It's the manufacturer's name," I said. "Annie got an amazing deal."

"I'll bet Gary wasn't pleased about that," she said. "He hates being outdone."

"You're telling me," Annie said. "He got so mad that he fired a kid named Tommy."

Della shook her head. "That's terrible, but truthfully, I told him that he should have quit months ago."

"You know him?" I asked.

"Of course I do. Gateway Lake is a small town. I shouldn't have to tell the two of you about how much interaction there is in tight communities. From what I understand, Maple Crest is much the same."

"It is," Annie conceded. "I hated to see it happen because of me, though."

"Don't worry yourself about it," Della said. "Tommy is destined for bigger and better things now that he's out from under Gary White's thumb."

"You know, Gary seemed so nice at first when we met him at the diner this morning, but we saw a completely different side of him at his store," I said as I pinched off a piece of ham.

"Patrick, at least get a plate," Annie scolded me.

"Fingers are fine, too," I answered, but I had to concede her point. "Are we waiting for someone else?"

"No, it's just the three of us," Della said.

"Then let's eat. I'm suddenly starving."

I grabbed a plate and started piling things on. I'd started off trying to choose in moderation, but there was just too much of it to do that.

"That was all delicious," I said as I pushed my plate aside. We'd eaten in her formal dining room, since there hadn't been any room in the kitchen or at the dinette. I never understood having a room devoted strictly to eating, but I was happy for it at the moment.

"I'm so glad you enjoyed it. I'm sure none of it was up to Annie's cast iron standards."

"Don't be so certain about that," I said, and my sister promptly swatted me. "Hey."

"I didn't hit you that hard," Annie said with a grin, "mostly because I agree with you."

"If you agree with me, then why did you swat me?"

"I like to keep you in line," my sister said with a smile.

"I really would love to taste some of your cast iron cooking sometime," Della said.

"I'd offer to make you something tonight, but I have a feeling that we'll be eating leftovers the entire time that we're here," Annie said as she picked up her plate and made her way back into the kitchen.

As we followed her with ours, Della said, "Don't worry about this spread. All of it will save nicely. I'd be honored if you'd make something for us tonight."

I'd seen the fire pit near the water the night before, and I had to admit, it would be the perfect spot to spend a few hours tending a fire, especially given the chill in the air. "Why not?" I asked my sister. "It could be fun."

"Really?" Annie asked me, clearly wanting to know if I was willing to put our investigation on hold while she cooked outdoors.

I nodded in agreement as I echoed, "Really." Since we were fresh out of ideas, it might be a nice experience to share.

"Let's do it, then. What sounds good to you, Aunt Della?" she asked.

"Oh, whatever you'd like to make would be delightful."

"I do my best. How about you, Pat?"

I thought about all of my sister's specialties, and then I finally came up with something I knew would be a hit. "You haven't made ribs in a while."

"I make them every week at the Iron," she reminded me.

"Maybe so, but usually they're all gone by the time I get around to eating," I replied. "I haven't had one of your ribs for months."

"Poor thing. I hadn't realized that you'd been so deprived."

"Well, now you know," I said with a grin.

"Ribs it is. Della, do you have any charcoal on hand?"

"No, and I'm afraid that I'm out of firewood as well, though Davis has offered some to me if I'm ever in need."

"Tell you what. Why don't I make enough food for all four of us?" Annie suggested. "We'll cook the food with charcoal and then eat by the campfire."

"It sounds wonderful to me. Shall I go to the store for you?" Della volunteered.

"We'll be happy to do that ourselves," I replied before Annie could answer. While we were out shopping, maybe we could get in a little more sleuthing along the way. If nothing else, we could discuss what the next day might bring, since it appeared that the active part of our investigation was over for the moment. That was the problem with everything that Della had told us so far. There was no way to prove or disprove that everything that had happened to her hadn't been just one string of coincidences.

"Would you like some help cleaning up before we go?" my sister asked.

"Would you mind? I don't really need any, but I'd love the company."

I was about to suggest to Annie that we didn't have that much time, but she answered before I had a chance to comment. "It would be fun, wouldn't it, Pat?"

"Sure," I said, knowing from my twin sister's tone of voice that the fight was over before the bell had even rung.

As we worked at clearing the table, Annie asked her, "Tell us what it was like growing up with Mom."

"She was the sweetest sister I could have ever asked for," Della said.

I knew for a fact that Mom, though normally tranquil, could still have a temper. "Come on, she wasn't all sunshine and light. You must have fought about a few things."

"Just Gregory Nance," she said promptly.

"Was he a high school sweetheart, by any chance?" Annie asked her.

"More like grade school," Della answered with a laugh. "I was two years older than your mother, and Greg was in class with her. She had a crush on him, but he set his sights for me instead. It was uncomfortable, to say the least, when Greg asked your mother if I had a boyfriend, and if not, did he have a chance? We didn't speak for three weeks, until Greg got a crush on another girl, Linda Perkins, and it all blew over. Other than that, she was my best friend growing up. We used to laugh about the oddest things that no one else found even remotely amusing."

It sounded as though she was describing Annie and me. I wasn't sure if it made me happy or sad, since Mom had died with a rift between them. I couldn't imagine turning my back on Annie, no matter what the circumstances. Then again, we'd shared a womb at the same time, so maybe we were different. Then again, maybe not.

"Excuse me," I said, suddenly not wanting to have anything to do with this particular conversation. "I need a little fresh air."

I walked out onto the front porch and sat on the top step.

In less than a minute, Annie came out and joined me. In a soft voice, she asked, "Pat, are you okay?"

"I'm fine," I said.

She sat down beside me anyway. "Don't lie to me, little brother. What's wrong?"

"Annie, promise me that won't ever happen to us," I said, the words just spilling out of me. "I couldn't bear the thought of not having you around."

"I swear," she said as she put an arm around me. "Like it or not, you're going to have me around forever, Pat. I can't imagine my life without you in it, and I know that you feel the same way about me."

"I'm sure that's what Mom and Della thought at one time, too."

To her credit, Annie didn't answer right away. "Yes, no doubt you're right, but we're not like that, and you know it."

"Because we're twins?" I asked her.

"That, and because our lives are so intertwined that I can't conceive of any circumstances that would split us up like that. Face it, Pat. We're stuck with each other, whether we like it or not."

I hugged her awkwardly for a moment, and then, to my surprise, I felt a tear trickling down my cheek. "Thanks. I needed that."

"You know, we don't have to talk about the past if it makes you so uncomfortable."

"No, it's fine. Really. I just started imagining my life without you in it. It was a gray and dreary place indeed."

"That's because I spread sunshine wherever I go," she said with a laugh. Annie stood and reached down to take my hand. "Now let's go back inside. I'm sure Della is worried that we've taken off on her."

"We can't do that, can we?" I suddenly didn't want to be in Gateway Lake, no matter how selfish that might make me. My sister and I were putting our lives in danger for a woman who was practically a stranger to us. She hadn't been a stranger to Mom, though. They'd shared their earlier lives together, and something, my father, had torn them apart.

Then again, if nothing else, we owed it to our late mother to figure out what was happening and try to stop it if we could.

"I don't really need to answer that, do I?" Annie asked.

"No, I understand why we're here." As we walked back inside, I said, "Sorry about that. I don't know what got into me."

"It's okay. You're entitled to show a little emotion every now and then. Just don't make a habit of it, okay?"

I laughed at her as I saluted. "I'll do my best."

"That's better," she said. "Now let's go finish cleaning up so we can make another big mess."

"That's the story of our lives, isn't it?"

CHAPTER 12: ANNIE

"T HIS IS GOING TO BE fun, Pat."

"That's because you love cooking," my brother said to me. "What am I supposed to be doing while you're making magic with cast iron?"

"First of all, thanks for the compliment, and secondly, you can tend the fire and keep me company. Once we have the coals going, I can do a quick seasoning on the Dutch oven, and then we'll be ready to cook. This is going to take the rest of the afternoon and evening, I'm afraid."

"Well, we really didn't have any plans going forward anyway, so why not enjoy the water view? How can Della afford to live on the lake like this?"

"She told me last night that she got the place at a foreclosure sale," I said.

"When did that conversation happen?" he asked me.

"We were upstairs getting ready for bed when I was wondering the same thing. Evidently the place was falling apart, but she dug in and turned it into something pretty wonderful. It must be great living on the water like this."

"Need I remind you that you live on a body of water yourself?" Pat asked.

"That's a pond, not a lake," I said. "It's completely different."

"Completely, or just a little?" he asked me with a grin.

"Completely," I confirmed. "The pond is tiny, but it's all mine. On the other hand, the lake is really a large span of water, but she shares it with countless other people. All kinds of interesting things happen here."

"I don't know. I kind of like your place better," he said.

"Coming from a city boy like you, that's a real compliment. You're not sorry I got the cabin in the woods and you're stuck in town, are you?"

"Are you kidding? I'd go crazy living out in the sticks like you do."

"And your apartment above the Iron would drive me nuts as well. I guess we're both suited for our lifestyles, aren't we?"

"It sounds like it to me. Do you mind making ribs this evening?" he asked.

"No, they're easier than a lot of things I make with cast iron," I said. "It will give us plenty of time to speculate about Della's situation a little more."

"It seems as though that's all that we've been doing, speculating," he said as I drove toward the supermarket. We had supplies to acquire before we could get started with prepping the cast iron and then cooking the meal.

"Do you honestly believe we've covered all that we need to discuss?" I asked him.

"Of course not, but it's feeling like circular logic to me. I just wish there was something more active that we could do."

I knew that our approach was frustrating to him. Shoot, it was aggravating me as well, but all we could do was ask questions, snoop around, look for clues, and try to figure out what was going on. We couldn't make people talk to us, and so far, our results had been mixed at best.

I wasn't about to give up, though.

There was too much at stake.

"Do you need some kind of a list?" Pat asked me as I pulled into the grocery store parking lot. It had been easy enough to find, given Della's directions and the small size of the town.

I tapped my forehead. "Nope, it's all up here."

"That's a scary thought," he said with a smile, and I was happy to see it. This case had thrown Pat off from the very start, and for some reason, dealing with Aunt Della had been much harder for him than it had been for me. I knew that I needed to make concessions to my brother's sensitivities without letting him know that I was doing it. I knew that Pat liked to think of himself as a man's man, and while I didn't think him having emotions precluded him from being called that, he might. It was up to me to support him in any way that I could, as long as it didn't jeopardize our investigation.

"Should I grab a buggy?" Pat asked me as we walked into the store.

"It might not be a bad idea," I said.

As he started to retrieve one of the green wired buggies from the queue, someone else was bringing one back into the store. "Would you like this one?" Henrietta Long asked me as she approached.

"Thanks, but Pat's grabbing one. Fancy running into you here."

"Gateway Lake isn't all that big," she said with a warm smile. "That's why it helps to get along with everyone. You never know when you'll see them again."

"I can't imagine you have any problems with that," I said to her.

"You'd be surprised," Henrietta said. In a lower voice, she added, "Some folks weren't all that happy with the job that Della and I did with the Winter Wonderland festivities."

"Funny, I thought it was a real success," Pat said as he joined us.

"Oh, a good time was had by all, there's no doubt about that, but the expenses were much more than we anticipated. I'm afraid that neither Della nor I are very good at business, though we know how to throw a party. We've been letting a few folks know that we aren't going to clear as much as we'd first hoped to soften the blow, but word is getting around town, and I have a feeling that things might get ugly. It's not just the financial paucity, though. I've already had complaints today about how Della handled things during the festivities."

"I thought you two worked together on everything?" I asked her. "Why would they single Della out?"

"Well, we were co-chairs, that's for sure, but we couldn't both do everything. I handled the finances mostly, while Della dealt with parade routes, booth allocations, and things like that. Not that her name wasn't on the bank account too, or that I didn't tweak a placement or two, but folks seem to be more upset with your aunt than they are with me. I do my best to defend her, but you know how people can be."

"Who in particular is unhappy about Della?" Pat asked.

"Oh, I don't feel right naming names," Henrietta said.

"We won't tell anyone that you told us," I reassured her. Pat and I needed information, and we were running into more dead ends than usual. Any enlightenment Henrietta could provide would be most appreciated.

"Well, I don't want to spread rumors, but Chief Cameron has been unhappy with her since she laughed at his dinner invitation. The man is positively obsessed with making her suffer some of the humiliation he felt from her rejection. Add Davis to the mix, who clearly has his sights set on her but is making no progress whatsoever, and you have the potential for things to get ugly there."

"So, these men really are infatuated with my aunt," Pat said.

"Oh, absolutely," Henrietta said. "Della has always been a looker, but she has an aura around her that most men our age find irresistible."

I smiled at the thought of grown men acting like teenagers trying to get the pretty girl's attention, until I remembered that a woman had been murdered. "What about Cheryl Simmons?"

"What about her? I don't know if any of the men had a crush on her too or not."

"Do you have any idea who might want to kill her?" Pat asked.

"No, it's baffling to me."

"Della believes that whoever killed Cheryl has been trying to kill her, too," I said.

Henrietta frowned. "Really? That possibility never crossed my mind. My lands, what is this world coming to?"

"You said earlier that people weren't happy with our aunt," I reminded Henrietta, who seemed a little scatterbrained.

"Did I?" she asked.

"Yes, you did. So far, you've mentioned the police chief and the mayor. Who does that leave, the candlestick maker?"

I'd been trying to be funny, but clearly Henrietta didn't get it. "I don't believe we have one of those in town, unless I'm mistaken." The puzzled look on her face amused me, but this wasn't the time or the place to smile.

"What I'm asking you is who else is upset with her? Is it Serena Jefferson, or perhaps Gary White by any chance?" Those names kept popping up in our investigation, and I was certain she was going to mention one of them.

She managed to surprise me, though. "No, the only other person I can think of offhand is Latham Gregg."

This was a new name to me. "Pardon me?"

"Latham," she said as she pointed in the direction of a man overseeing the cashiers at the checkout lines. He was in his late fifties, with a full head of snowy-white hair and a belly that would make him the perfect candidate to play Santa around Christmastime. "He runs this place, though I heard he might lose his job, all because of Della."

"What could our aunt possibly have to do with him being fired?" Pat asked.

"Didn't you know? Latham was supposed to sponsor the festivities, but at the last minute, Della canceled his participation out of nowhere. It was a real black mark against the store, and the owner is threatening to get rid of him because of it."

"Why did Della change her mind?" I asked her.

"I only wish that I knew. You'll have to ask her. When I tried to talk some sense into her, she refused to give me an answer that made any kind of sense at all. We were counting on that money to break even. Honestly, I don't know what we're going to do now." She lowered her voice again as she said, "Shhh. Here he comes."

The grocery store manager walked over to us and frowned at Henrietta for a moment before offering my brother and me a smile. "Hello, folks. Was there something I could help you with?"

"We're just here to do a little shopping," I told him.

"These are Della's people, Latham," Henrietta said. "This is Annie, and this is Pat."

I don't know why she'd felt the need to make introductions, especially since it was clear that Latham was not all that pleased to learn of our local connections. "Nice to meet you," he said perfunctorily. "If we can help in any way, be sure to ask one of our associates."

He started to walk away when Pat said, "We'd love to know the real reason why our aunt cancelled your involvement with Winter Wonderland at the last minute, if you wouldn't mind sharing the information with us."

Henrietta's face went white. "Latham, I don't know where they heard about that, but I didn't say a word." She looked at Pat as though she wanted to choke him on the spot, an emotion I felt myself occasionally. I was surprised that my brother had taken such a direct approach, but since he'd opened that particular can of worms, I had no choice but to chime in myself.

"Believe me, we understand Aunt Della can be difficult at times," I said, "but anything you could tell us might be useful."

Henrietta glanced at her watch before the grocery manager could reply. "Is that the time already? I really must be going."

The woman shot out of there so quickly she could have been on wheels.

"Ask your aunt," Latham said coldly after Henrietta was gone.

"We will, but right now, we're asking you," I said.

"Fine. It's no secret. I told Della that for the money she was demanding, I expected more of a push from the festival. She told me that I was being ridiculous and that she was doing me a favor by even allowing the store to be a sponsor. I'm not proud of it, but I lost my temper, and I told her she could go howl at the moon if that was the way she felt about it. Della took out our contract and tore it up right in front of me. I knew that I'd made a mistake and let my feelings get the better of me, but when I asked her to reconsider, she flatly refused.

She had our store name pulled from every bit of advertising and told me that she'd be refunding my contributions as soon as they balanced the books for the event. When my boss found out, she went ballistic, and if I don't increase store profits, and quickly, I'm on my way out. That aunt of yours is as stubborn as a mule, if you'll pardon me for saying so."

"No need to apologize. It runs in our family," I said. "You must have been really angry with her."

"Well, I wasn't happy with her, if that's what you're asking," Latham said.

"Were you mad enough to kill her?" Pat asked him quietly.

"What? No! Of course not."

"I'm curious about something. When exactly did all of this happen?" I asked him.

"It was on the morning of the parade," he admitted. "You wouldn't believe how quickly she had our store logo removed from the main float, let alone the places it was posted around the town supper."

"Thanks for talking to us so candidly about it. We're sorry to keep you," I said. "I know you must be busy."

"Yes, I have my hands full at the moment," he said. "Don't worry, I won't hold your aunt's behavior against you if you don't hold mine against me," he said with a sad smile.

"Consider it done," I said.

Once Latham was back at the registers, Pat asked, "Why did you let him off the hook so easily, Sis?"

"He's not the one we're after," I said.

"How can you be so sure?"

"The first attempt on Della's life was the plummeting snowman, and that happened the day before the parade," I said. "That's long before Latham and our aunt had their blowout fight."

"What if that part was coincidence, but the rest of it was him trying to get rid of her?" Pat asked me.

"I suppose that it's possible, but can we really pick and choose the

Motive

attempts to make them match our theories? I say we keep our eye on him, but he can't go on our main list."

"I can live with that," Pat said. "Man oh man, can you believe that?"

"Which part?"

"Well, we already knew that our aunt had a quick temper, but that seemed downright reckless even for her, cancelling the store's involvement at the last minute like that. It must have killed their last chance of making a profit," he answered.

"I don't know what to tell you. Let's go shopping."

In short order, we had charcoal briquettes, barbeque sauce, onions, carrots, green peppers, and olive oil. Going to the meat department, all we needed now were the ribs.

There were none in the display case.

I rang a bell by the window that led into the back, and a pretty young woman in her early twenties came out from the back. She was dressed in a white apron and wore a cute little white hat as well. Her name tag said that she was STACI, with an I. I wasn't sure what I'd been expecting, but certainly not her.

"May I help you?"

"I see you are out of ribs," I said.

"Pork or beef?" she asked.

"Pork."

"Full or baby back?"

"Baby back," I said.

"How many people are you feeding?"

"Four, maybe five," I said.

"Give me a second," she said with a grin. "I'll be right back."

Two minutes later, Staci came back carrying a large black foam tray, shrink-wrapped and loaded with my requested ribs. "Here you go."

"Thanks. Do you mind if I ask you a personal question, Staci?"

"Go ahead. If I don't like it, I'll just ignore it," she replied with a grin.

"How long have you been a butcher?" I asked out of curiosity.

"Oh, this isn't my profession. It's more of a hobby, really."

Pat laughed beside me. "Really? It's an interesting hobby to have."

"For a girl, you mean?" she asked without a hint of malice in her voice.

"More like for someone your age," Pat said.

"I'm not at all certain that's any better," Staci answered, still smiling. "Dad's the butcher here normally, but he's off hunting with my uncles, so I'm filling in. Usually I'm a dental hygienist at Dr. Pickering's office, but she's off this week as well, so I was free."

"Is she hunting, too?"

"Maybe for a suntan in the Caribbean," the girl said, laughing. "Dad wanted a son to join him in the trade, but my brother had no interest in the profession. Me, I took to it immediately. You should have seen me dissecting a frog in biology class. I've never been squeamish, so Dad offered to teach me, and I was happy just spending time with him." She laughed. "That's way more than you need to know, isn't it? Enjoy those ribs."

"We will," I said as Pat and I walked away.

"I just love small towns," he said. "You meet the most interesting people."

"You can meet them in big cities, too," I said.

"Maybe so, but they don't often slow down long enough to tell you their life stories, especially over raw meat."

"I guess that all depends on who you run into," I answered. "Most folks have an interesting story to tell. They're just not as open to sharing them as Staci is."

"Then more folks should be like her," Pat said. "Now, should we buy this stuff and head back to Della's place?"

"We'd better. I have to do a preliminary seasoning on the Dutch oven before I start cooking with it, so we'd better get started if there's any hope that we're going to be eating tonight."

"I vote for eating. Always. Not eating isn't even an option, as far as I'm concerned."

"Then let's get to it."

CHAPTER 13: PAT

"**D**O YOU MIND IF WE stop by the mayor's office on the way back to Della's?" I asked Annie after we loaded up our groceries.

"Why, do you want to get in another round of questioning before we start getting ready for dinner tonight?" she asked.

"No, but we're going to need firewood for the seasoning, and I'd feel better asking him directly, even though Della said we had his permission. Besides, we still have to invite him to the meal," I reminded her.

Annie looked at the clock on the dashboard before she answered me. "We can stop, but we can't talk too long. I need to marinate the ribs, season the Dutch oven, and then get started on dinner."

"It shouldn't take long," I assured her. I wasn't about to get into another lengthy interview session if I could avoid it, but a lot of that depended on Davis and Serena. At least we didn't have to worry about the meat going bad in the car. The temperature outside was cold enough to keep it safe for as long as we needed it to be.

When Annie and I walked into the mayor's office in city hall, I was surprised to find Chief Cameron in deep conversation with Serena, the mayor's secretary. For the life of me, it appeared that the two of them were conspiring together about something, exchanging whispers.

"Are we interrupting something?" I asked them both.

The police chief frowned the moment he saw us, but Serena's reaction was more interesting. She began to blush, and then she tried to stammer out an explanation. "We were just...talking."

"We could see that," I said. "Was it about anything interesting?"

"You don't have to tell him anything, Serena," Chief Cameron told her.

"It's not important. Chief, if you're here to see the mayor, we'd be glad to wait our turn," Annie said with her brightest and most insincere smile.

"No, thanks. I was just on my way out," the police chief said. "Speaking of which, how long are you two planning on staying in Gateway Lake?"

"Why, do we need permission to hang around?" I asked him.

"Of course not. I know you need to get back to your store," he said, "and I'd hate for something to happen to it while you were away."

"No worries on that account," I said, trying not to show any reaction to his tone of voice. "The place is in good hands."

"Okay, then," he said, and then he left, but not before he whispered something to Serena that I couldn't quite make out.

"I didn't realize you two were an item," Annie asked her after the police chief was gone. "How long have you been dating?"

"We're not dating," she said a little indignantly. "What gave you that idea?"

"The fact that he was so protective of you just makes it look that way," I said. I didn't believe it any more than Annie did, but if we got Serena flustered, maybe she'd disclose something she wouldn't want us to know.

"Cam is just a friend," Serena said. After biting her lower lip for a moment, she said, "I'm afraid the mayor is awfully busy at the moment, but I'd be glad to pencil you in for sometime next week, if you'd like to come back."

Before I could respond, Davis walked out of his office. "I thought I heard voices out here. Wasn't Chief Cameron just here?"

"He left just a second ago. We thought he came by to see you," I said.

"No, not that I know of," the mayor said. "What brings you two by my office?"

"Mr. Mayor, don't forget, you have that meeting with the Women's Auxiliary."

Davis glanced at his watch. "That's not for half an hour. I have plenty of time to speak with these folks. Why don't you both come into my office?"

"This won't take long," I assured him. "We're here to invite you to a cookout tonight at Della's place."

"I'd be delighted to come," he said, accepting before learning a single detail about the invitation. "Is there something I can bring?"

"How about firewood?" Annie asked. "We're cooking ribs outside in a cast iron Dutch oven."

"So, you need the wood for cooking," he said.

"No, we're using charcoal for that, but a fire would be useful for seasoning the iron. Besides, it will make it nicer for us as we cook, and Aunt Della did say that you made the offer earlier in the year."

"Sure, grab all you want. It's stacked up under the back deck, but you're welcome to all that you can carry," he said. "What time should I come by for the meal?"

"When you smell the ribs cooking, it's time to come on over. If you need a more precise time than that, I'd say sometime around six would be fine," Annie said.

"I'll be there," he said, and then his cellphone rang. After glancing to see who was calling him, he said, "Sorry, but I have to get this."

After Davis walked back into his office, deep in conversation, he shut his door.

"That sounds like fun," Serena said, trying to appear nonchalant.

"What's that?" I asked her.

"A barbeque. I've never had cast iron ribs before. I bet they're delicious."

It was clearly a request for an invitation, but I wasn't sure that we'd have enough food if she came. Besides, the dynamic might be a little odd if Della, the mayor, and his secretary were all there at the same time. I was about to say no when Annie surprised me.

"Sure, the more the merrier. Come by around six."

I gave my sister an odd look, but before I could withdraw Annie's invitation, she said, "I hate to just run off, but we'd better go. If you'd like to bring something, how about a dessert? Make it something decadent, okay?"

"I can do that," she said, smiling at my sister.

Once we were back out at Annie's car, I asked, "Would you mind telling me what that was all about?"

"Pat, there will be plenty of food. Don't worry about it."

"I'm not worried about the amount of food I'm going to get," I said. "Really?"

"Well, not just that. Why did you invite her?"

"How could we not?" Annie asked. "We can see firsthand how Serena reacts to Della and Davis together. I would have invited the police chief too if I'd thought about it when we saw him."

"There's still time," I said sarcastically.

"You're right. Let's go find his office. It's in the basement, isn't it?"

"Are you serious?"

"Come on. Let's make it a party. Do you think Gary White will come, too?"

"That's where I'm drawing the line. Even with the police chief, we'll have more people than we know what to do with."

"Maybe you'll get lucky and he'll turn our invitation down," Annie said.

No such luck, though. To my surprise and my sister's delight, the police chief accepted as well. He hadn't even had to mull it over.

"We're going to need a bigger Dutch oven," I said as we walked out to Annie's car.

"Don't forget, Aunt Della made a ton of food for lunch today. We can have a buffet *and* a campfire. Who knows? Maybe it will loosen some tongues if we bring out some wine, too."

"You never know," I said. "All of a sudden this has turned into a major production."

"No worries, little brother. It will be fun."

"I didn't realize that we were doing this for our own amusement," I told her.

"No, but it's nice if it's a bonus, don't you think?"

———————

We got back to Della's, and while Annie took the food inside to start the marinating process with the ribs and barbeque sauce, I went next door to Davis's place to get the promised firewood.

What I found under the mayor's deck put our bonfire plans on hold, maybe indefinitely.

———————

I could tell from the first glance that one piece of wood was different from the rest. Every other piece under the deck was split and seasoned firewood, but one was a rounded limb three inches thick, twice as long as the other pieces, and still green and covered with bark. I picked it up and was ready to throw it toward the back of the pile under the deck when I noticed two things about the limb: it had bits of hair clinging to one end of it, as well as some kind of manmade fabric strands.

Were the police wrong about what had knocked Cheryl Simmons out?

Was *this* the murder weapon instead of the flashlight they believed had been used?

———————

"Annie, I need you right now," I said when I called my sister next door.

"Can it wait? I'm almost finished marinating the ribs."

"Rome is burning," I said, our cue that something was indeed very wrong.

"Are you at Davis's house?" she asked me, her voice suddenly cold.

"Yes."

"I'll be right there."

My sister was as good as her word. Twenty seconds later, I heard Annie calling out from nearby, "Pat? Are you okay?"

"I'm fine," I said.

She climbed beneath the deck, which was about four feet off the ground. Annie had to stoop over, but I was hunchbacked where I was. "What is it, Pat? What's wrong?"

I showed her the length of wood in my hand. "Do you see what I see?"

I loved that my sister was so quick. "That's what somebody used on Cheryl Simmons, not Aunt Della's flashlight."

"I agree. The real question is what should we do with it?"

"We have to tell Chief Cameron," Annie said firmly.

"Do we? Are you absolutely sure about that?"

She frowned at me before she spoke again. "Pat, we can't obstruct justice. This could be important."

"We don't even know with any certainty what it is," I said.

"No, but we both have a pretty good idea, don't we?"

"Is that enough, though? I agree, we need to tell the police chief about this. My question is, do we have to do it this exact second?"

"Are we going to just leave it here and pretend that we didn't find it?" Annie asked me.

"Of course not. We're taking it with us. I'm not going to take the chance that the killer might come back for it. At least not yet."

"You have a plan, don't you?"

"It's more of an inkling at this point, Annie. We may be able to use this to our advantage, but if we turn it over to Cameron, we're giving up the first real edge we've had since we started digging into this."

"What if it could help him solve the murder?" my sister asked me.

"What if he's the killer himself?" I countered.

"Do you honestly believe that the chief of police was stupid enough to throw this branch under here instead of straight in the water?"

"Who knows? Maybe something startled him, and he had to suddenly run from the murder scene. Throwing this into the water would just call attention to it, and he surely wouldn't want to be caught with it red handed. What better place to hide a piece of wood than among other pieces of wood?"

"If he's the one who did it, he's going to suspect we found it, given the fact that we're about to have a fire, and it isn't here any more. Doesn't that say we should leave it right here?"

"Again, I don't want to take the chance of losing it. Is taking it ideal? No, but what choice do we have? This could be the piece of evidence that helps catch a killer."

"I have another thought," Annie said.

"I'd love to hear it."

"I think I saw more wood like this when we walked the lake path last night. Let's go check it out."

"Should I just leave this here then?" I asked her as I gestured with the limb still in my hands.

"No, you're right. Until we figure out what we're going to do, we need to keep an eye on it. Bring it with us."

I wasn't sure that I wanted to be seen carrying the murder weapon around in my hands. "How about if I store it somewhere no one will be able to find it?" I asked her.

"Where can you do that?"

"We could always put it in the back of your car," I suggested. "At least that way we'd be able to lock it up."

I could tell Annie wasn't too thrilled with my plan, but when she couldn't come up with another one on the spur of the moment, she agreed. I grabbed her car keys and put the wood in back, pulling the cover over it so no one could see it if they happened to glance in the back. The Subaru didn't have a trunk, per se, more of a cargo space, but there was a cover that retracted which we could use to hide what I'd just found. It felt good getting it out of my hands, and I wiped them both on my jeans subconsciously, trying to get rid of the taint of death from them.

"I'll follow you," I said when I got back to Annie, and we started walking down the path we'd taken the night before. I hadn't spotted any wood on the side of the way, but then again, I hadn't been holding the flashlight, either. Sure enough, between us and the crime scene tape, some thick branches had been recently cut to clear the path a little. It was obvious that the piece I'd just hidden in Annie's car had come from this cutting.

Annie reached down and picked up another piece that came close to matching the murder weapon in length and diameter. "Here's what we'll do. We put this where you found the other one, and if the killer comes back for it, he won't be suspicious about its absence."

"Only this one's missing hair and fiber samples," I said.

"They aren't going to be looking at it that closely. What do you think?"

"It sounds like a good plan to me. I'll feel better once we get this back in the other one's place, grab our firewood, and get away from that deck altogether."

"Me, too," Annie said as we walked back toward Davis's place in single file.

We almost made it without being seen.

The key word was "almost."

CHAPTER 14: ANNIE

"WHAT ARE YOU TWO UP to?" a voice called out from ahead of us on the lake loop path.

I nearly dropped the wood in my hand when I saw that it was Chief Cameron. Without a word, my brother stepped in front of me, allowing me to be shielded for a moment before the chief could see us clearly. At least we'd been coming around the bend, and thus out of his sight, before he'd called out. The branch in my hand was large and heavy, and not at all easy to shove into my pocket. I couldn't let the police chief see me with it, though. There was only one thing I could do. I hiked up Pat's jacket, shoved the branch under it, and then I tucked the edge of it down his pants. He jerked a little, and I knew that the bark must have taken off a little skin, but to his credit, he didn't cry out.

"Hello, Chief," I said as I stepped out from behind my brother. "We decided to take a little walk before we started working on dinner. I'm so glad that you'll be joining us."

"With all of my suspects gathered together, how could I refuse?" he asked, still watching us both suspiciously. "That's why you're doing this, isn't it? You want to get everyone together like some kind of mystery from the forties and name the killer."

"You're reading way too much into it. We're just having a meal," I said.

"Sure. I believe you," he said in such a way that it was clear that he didn't trust us at all.

"See for yourself this evening," Pat said. "By the way, what are *you* doing out here? I figured you'd be busy working on your case."

"I am. I keep thinking that we're missing something, so I decided to walk the path from Della's to the spot where Cheryl was murdered to see if there's anything I might have missed. You two haven't seen anything, have you?"

It was the perfect time to come clean with him, but I wasn't about to do it, and I knew that Pat was just as reticent as I was about sharing our recent find. Was Chief Cameron really out looking for clues, or had he come to retrieve the murder weapon? If so, he'd already found that it was missing, and we had to be his main suspects, given our proximity to the deck.

"No, not so much," Pat said. I knew without even glancing at my brother that he was thinking the same thing I was. This man could be extremely dangerous to us, and we might have inadvertently tipped our hand without realizing it. If he'd seen the branch in my hand before I'd managed to hide it under my brother's jacket, we'd both just drawn targets on our backs. The police chief may have just been one of several of our suspects, but he was certainly the most well-armed one.

"We need to get to work if we're all going to be eating in time, so we'll see you this evening," I said as he walked past us. He glanced back at Pat, but I'd maneuvered myself to block the chief's view of the bulge in my brother's back.

"See you then," he said as he moved on, scouring the path in front of him, at least pretending to look for something significant. Before Cameron turned the corner, I saw him glance back in our direction out of the corner of my eye, but Pat was pointing to some nonexistent object out on the water, and I pretended to be mesmerized by it. The police chief followed our glances, but he clearly couldn't see our imaginary focus point, and he quickly moved away out of sight.

"That was quick thinking," Pat said as he retrieved the branch from his jacket.

"Sorry if I scraped some skin jamming it back there," I said.

"Hey, I'm just glad he didn't see what we were up to. He didn't, did he?"

"I wish I could say for sure, but I think we're in the clear," I said. "That depends on whether he hadn't already checked under the mayor's deck for the murder weapon, that is."

"Have we suddenly decided that Chief Cameron is the killer?" Pat asked me curiously.

"No, I don't have any real reason to think that, at least not any more than I do the others, but it does seem rather suspicious that he shows up here at this moment, just after you discover what was really used to send Cheryl Simmons tumbling into the lake."

"Then again, he might just be telling the truth, and he's out looking for clues like he said he was."

"If that's the case, then we just deprived him of finding anything, didn't we?"

"For now," Pat said. "Are you having doubts about our plan?"

"No, but we should keep an eye on our guests and see if any of them venture under Davis's deck while we're not looking."

"I can do that," Pat said. "I'll plant this branch back where I found the other one and grab some firewood while I'm down there. Are you about ready to start seasoning that iron, or did I interrupt you too soon?"

"No, I was just about finished with the marinade, and Aunt Della offered to put it in the fridge for me when I left to join you."

"What excuse did you make for leaving so abruptly?" my brother asked me.

"I told her you dropped your wallet somewhere, and I was going to help you look for it," I said apologetically. "Sorry. I didn't mean to make you sound like a dolt."

"It could have been a whole lot worse. You could have said that I lost my pants."

"I'll save that for next time," I said with a grin.

"What makes you think there's going to be a next time?" he asked me with a smile of his own.

"Face it. With us, there's *always* going to be a next time," I replied. "Build a good fire. I need some hot coals to get the iron up to temperature."

"I'm on it," Pat said.

We parted ways after I helped him carry a load of wood from Davis's place to Aunt Della's. Pat was starting the fire as I ducked inside, only to find Aunt Della standing at the back door staring at me.

What was this about, I wondered?

⊷❦⊶

"Did you find it?" she asked me.

For a moment I panicked, forgetting what excuse I'd used to get away from her so quickly. Then it came back to me. "We sure did. It turned out to be the last place we looked."

"Well, I certainly hope so, else why would you keep looking?" she asked. "I need to ask you something."

Oh, no. Had she seen what we'd done? I hadn't realized it, but from where we were standing, my aunt had a perfect view of the path below us, right where I'd jammed that branch up Pat's jacket and down his pants. "Fine," I said, trying to keep my expression neutral as I gathered up the Dutch oven's top and pot, the olive oil, a hot pad, and a roll of paper towels.

"Annie, how many people did you invite tonight?" she asked me.

It was all I could do not to show my relief upon hearing her question. "We'll have a minimum of four, and a maximum of seven."

"Seven people? I'm worried that there won't be enough food," she protested.

"We can all share, and if we need more, we can always dip into the leftovers from lunch," I explained.

"Well, we certainly can't eat outside, given the number of guests we'll be feeding," Aunt Della said. "The picnic table won't hold that many, and besides, where are we going to put all of the food? Can't you cook the ribs inside?"

"I could, but I like them better cooked in coals outside," I said. I

118

really did prefer that method, but it wasn't why I was pushing for it at the moment. I wanted our suspects to be tempted by Davis's firewood. If someone kept glancing over there, it might tell us something. Then again, if they made it a point to never look in that direction at all, that could tell us something as well. Dining inside was not in my plans.

Evidently I didn't have the final say in the matter, though. "I'm not at all sure that's going to work out," Aunt Della said as she looked around. "If we add the leaves to my table, we'll have plenty of room, and there's space on the island to pile up the food. Besides, it's going to be too chilly outside to have a picnic."

"But we've already…"

I was interrupted by my aunt's hand being held up in the air. "It's already been decided, Annie. You may cook out there if you'd like, but we're eating inside, and that's final."

"I suppose that would be fine," I said as I headed for the door.

Aunt Della glanced at the clock. "Surely it's too early to start cooking now."

"Not as early as you think, but the truth of the matter is that I still need to season the cookware before we get started."

"Doesn't it come preseasoned?" she asked.

"The new stuff does, but this is all vintage cookware. I need some time to build up a little seasoning, or everything's going to stick to the bottom." I could have cheated by using too much oil and layering the veggies, but I couldn't bring myself to do that to vintage Griswold cast iron. As it was, I was pushing things quite a bit, but I didn't have six hours to bake the pot's seasoning in Aunt Della's oven. Besides, the process would have filled the house with a smell that I doubted my aunt would appreciate. It wasn't exactly a burning odor as the oil baked into the iron, but to the unappreciative, it probably didn't smell all that great, either.

"Very well, but at least take some mittens with you," she said as she tried to shove a pair into my hands.

"Thanks, but I have my own gloves." I hadn't worn mittens since kindergarten, and I didn't even realize they made them in my size.

Pat had a nice fire going outside when I joined him, and he'd managed to already begin building up a lovely set of coals. "Well done."

"Don't give me too much credit," he said with a grin. "This is some pretty awesome firewood."

"Nothing but the best for the mayor, right?" I asked. I would season the outside of the pan later, but right now, I needed to take care of the inside. I'd already wiped the dust from all of the surfaces, so I took some oil and spread it thinly using a paper towel on the bottom and sides of the pot. The top would get a light coat before the first bake, but that could wait. After I wiped off the excess with a clean paper towel, I nestled the pan into the coals, allowing the metal to heat up slowly as it absorbed the oil. In five minutes, the surface oil was gone, so I added another small dollop, being careful to spread it around again. There was no puddling yet, which meant I was doing a good job adding thin layers at a time. Some folks tried to speed up the process by adding enough oil to choke the pores of the metal. That led to too much oil on the surface and not enough absorbed into the pot, and nothing good ever came from that. I kept up the process for half an hour, watching things carefully. After I was satisfied that I had a good start, I wiped out the last of the oil and, using the paper towel, I wiped the top of the lid's surface as well. Placing the oven back on the coals with its lid in place, I had Pat add some on top as well to give us a nice even bake.

"There, that should do for the next hour, and then we'll do it once more," I said.

"Will two seasonings be enough?" Pat asked me. We were both good with cast iron, but by virtue of our jobs back at the Iron, I had more daily exposure to cooking with cast iron, whereas Pat kept up with everything else we handled. I would have a tough time running the register up front, especially making the final report and balancing the books, but I could do it in a pinch, which described my brother's cast iron care and maintenance abilities as well.

"It's not perfect, but it should be okay," I said. "I still feel guilty about how we got this iron."

"Hey, you paid the asking price on the Dutch oven and the skillet," Pat said. "You shouldn't beat yourself up about that."

"I'm talking about getting Tommy fired," I said.

"He said it himself. You probably did him a favor."

"I suppose so. Did you ever imagine that Gary White could turn out to be so mean after how nice he was when we first met him?"

"You never know with some folks," Pat said. "He's got himself a temper, there's no doubt about that."

"I know, but could he have gotten mad enough to try to kill Aunt Della just because she wouldn't alter the parade route?" I asked my brother. "It just doesn't seem reasonable."

"How about all of those road rage incidents we keep hearing about?" Pat countered. "Do those acts of violence seem logical and well thought out to you?"

"No, I see what you're saying. I just can't buy him trying to kill her so passively, though."

"What do you mean?" Pat asked as he stoked the fire to the side where his feeding coals were coming from. He was really good at tending a fire, but what man wasn't a little boy at heart when it came to dancing flames? Every man I knew reverted to their youth given a hearty fire and a stick to prod it with.

"The snowman off the roof doesn't seem like a rage-driven attempt, does it?"

Pat thought about that for a second before he answered. "No, but it could have just been an accident. Those snowmen are bulky. Who could have possibly thought that putting a few of them on the bank roof was a good idea?"

"I know. They must have gotten caught up in the spirit of the festivities. Don't quote me, but given Aunt Della and Henrietta, it's amazing the whole thing came off as well as it did."

"They make quite the pair," Pat said, adding another small chunk of wood to the fire. "It's no wonder the operation is in the red, though. I hope folks had fun at the festivities, because from the sound of it, that's all anyone's going to get out of it."

"Let's get back to the attempted murders. Even if we assume that the falling snowman was an accident, how about the idea that someone pushed Aunt Della out in front of the fire truck?"

"Again, people get jostled watching parades all of the time," Pat answered. "It could have easily just been another accident."

"Are you starting to have doubts about what we're doing here?" I asked my brother. "Is there the slightest chance that you're thinking that this is all in Aunt Della's head after all?"

"No, I'm not saying that at all. Cheryl Simmons is dead, and someone tried to get into the house last night after we all went to bed. I'm not about to discount either one of those things. I'm just saying that they *all* might not be related to attempts on her life."

"What about the food poisoning?" I asked him.

"If that was attempted murder, it was botched pretty badly. Evidently Della wasn't even that sick from it, and there's no proof that there was anything wrong with her food in the first place."

"Maybe not, but it's awfully convenient that her plate was gone when she came back from the restroom, so there was no way to tell for sure one way or the other."

"It's like most of the other attempts she's faced," Pat said. "They could have *all* been earnest, for all we know. Then again, some of them could have just been coincidences."

"But at this point, we have no way of separating fact from fancy," I said. "What about our other suspects? Do any of the attempts fit *any* of them?"

"Well, the mayor was the one who saved Della at the parade, so that should clear him," Pat answered.

"It was a good thing he was standing nearby."

"Was it?" Pat asked as though something had suddenly occurred to him. "Annie, what if Davis gave her the push himself, but then he was worried that someone might have seen it happen? That would give him the opportunity to shove her and then just as much reason to grab her before she was hurt."

"As far as we know, he could have made all of those attempts on her life," I said as I brushed the coals away before I used the jack handle Pat had brought from my car for me to use as a lid lifter. It wasn't technically meant to do the job, nor were the hammers or crowbars that I often used back home, but it worked fine for our purposes. The olive oil had been well absorbed, with very little residue remaining. I decided that it was time to give the interior surfaces a second coat of olive oil and another baking session. As I worked, I continued talking. "There's one thing that bothers me about that theory. Davis wouldn't be stupid enough to throw the murder weapon under his own deck, would he?" I asked Pat as I settled the pot back onto the fire.

As he piled more coals on the top, my brother replied, "What better place to hide it than there? No one would be under there but him."

"But he told us we could grab all of the wood we wanted this afternoon," I reminded my brother.

"Yes, that's a point, but maybe he was taking a calculated risk that we wouldn't notice it. If that's the case, he's going to be pretty relieved this evening when no mention is made of the firewood."

"We might be able to use that to our advantage," I said.

"How's that?"

"Let's wait until everyone is gathered around the table, and then we'll make it a point to thank Davis for the use of his firewood from under his deck. If anyone reacts, we'll have ourselves a solid suspect."

"It's risky though, isn't it?" Pat asked.

"What's not in what we're doing? It's worth a shot, isn't it?"

"I'm game if you are," he said. "It won't be the first time we put ourselves out there as bait."

"And yet I never get used to the idea," I said with a smile. "So, Gary White is less likely as a suspect, while Davis is more of a possibility than we'd realized before. What about Chief Cameron?"

"I like him for it," Pat said. "Don't ask me why. There's just something about the man that I don't trust."

"But you don't have any concrete reasons to feel that way," I said.

"No, not a one, but he's got to be on our list."

"Agreed. How about Serena Jefferson?"

"I can see the snowman, the shove, and the poison, but I'm not at all sure she could club Cheryl from behind," Pat said.

"Why not? Women are just as capable of violent crime as men. It's turned into an equal-opportunity world."

"I'm not saying that a woman couldn't have done it. I'm just not sure that Serena did."

"Pat, you've got a dangerous blind spot there. No matter what we've seen in the past, you still hate thinking of women as being capable of murder, and it might end up biting you on the rear one of these days."

"That's why I've got you," he said with a sheepish grin. "It's your job to keep me focused and in line."

"I'm not sure I'm up for a task as daunting as that," I said with a laugh, "but I'll try. Have we forgotten anyone?"

"Well, I know that we ruled out the grocery store manager, but he's still a possibility if there's backstory there that we're not aware of. Besides him, I can't think of anyone else. Do you have any dark horses that you like?"

"No," I said. "I think we've covered all of our bases." I scraped off the coals again, checked the interior of the pot, and then I took the whole thing off the fire. "I think we're ready."

"Excellent," Pat said. "Do you still want to use the charcoal we bought?"

"Yes, just so we can be sure that we get an even heat. I don't want to take any chances with so much company coming."

"Then I'll get the briquettes ready while you go get the food," he said.

CHAPTER 15: PAT

B Y THE TIME ANNIE HAD everything prepped in the house, I had the briquettes firing up at a nice white glow outside. Scraping aside the burning chunks of wood from our earlier fire toward the edge of the pit, I spread some of the coals in a rough circle the size of the Dutch oven's perimeter. "What's the ratio top to bottom you like?" I asked my sister as she approached.

"How many did you make to start with?"

"Twenty briquettes," I said, doing a quick count.

Doing a quick calculation in her head, she said, "Put eight below and twelve on top. Heat rises, you know, so we need more coals on top than we do on the bottom."

"Yes, ma'am, I'm well aware of that fact," I said as I made sure I had eight pieces of charcoal in place, and then I put the empty oven over the top of them. Now it was up to Annie to build the meal inside the pot before I could place the lid and add the rest of the charcoal to the top. She took thick slabs of onion, green pepper, and chunks of carrots and spread them out on the bottom. Then she added half a cup of water, along with a few spices she'd mixed in, and finally, the ribs went on top, bone side down. Coating them with half the sauce in the bottle, Annie smiled at me as she wiped her hands on a nearby paper towel. "We're all set."

I placed the lid on top, and then I spread the twelve remaining coals around on top of the lid. Once we had everything in place, Annie said, "We'll need twenty more in about an hour."

I set the timer on my cellphone. "What do we do in the meantime?"

"The first thing I'm going to do is to wash my hands properly in the sink," Annie said. "We don't really have to baby this meal. There's no wind to speak of, and the outdoor temperature seems to be holding pretty steady."

"How's the barometric pressure doing?" I asked her with a smile.

"You laugh, but just about anything can affect the way food cooks outdoors."

"I'm just teasing. Why don't you go in, and I'll stay out here and mind the fire?"

"Pat, you know that it wouldn't kill you to spend a little of your free time with Aunt Della."

"You're probably right, but why take the chance?" I grinned to show that I was teasing, but I could tell that I'd pushed Annie a little too far. I'd have to back off unless I wanted another lecture, one for a class I hadn't remembered signing up for in the first place. Fortunately, I was saved by my cellphone's ring, and I was delighted to see that it was Jenna. "Sorry, I have to take this."

Annie laughed after I showed her who was calling. "Saved by the bell."

"I couldn't have planned it any better myself," I said. After I answered the call, I said, "Hey, stranger. How are things in Maple Crest?"

"Well, I'm up to my eyebrows in cows at the moment," she said with a hint of laughter in her voice. Only a vet would find that amusing.

"Wow, that sounds like a lot of cows."

"To be fair, it doesn't take a lot of them to be surrounded. I'm waiting for the farmer to grab something for me, so I thought I'd give you a call and see how your investigation is going." Jenna loved being a veterinarian, and she was usually the one who was too busy to talk between the two of us, so it was nice getting a call from her.

"It's going, however slowly."

"How's your aunt? Are things okay on that front? I know when you left you weren't quite sure how you were going to be able to handle that situation."

It was a sweet way of asking how I was dealing with my long-absent aunt, but I really didn't want to get into it over the phone. Instead, I deflected by saying, "She's doing okay, but her best friend was found murdered yesterday, so there's that."

"That's terrible!" Jenna said. "What happened?"

"The woman was struck from behind. It wasn't enough to kill her, but it did render her unconscious. After that happened, evidently she rolled into the lake and drowned."

"I can't imagine how awful that must be. Your aunt must be beside herself with grief."

"You know what? She's really not," I said, not fully realizing the fact until that moment. "She was pretty choked up about it yesterday, but today she seems as though she's handling it just fine. She should still be torn up, shouldn't she? Especially since she believes that the killing blow was meant for her all along."

"Why on earth would she think that?" Jenna asked me.

"Cheryl, that's her friend, was wearing Della's jacket at night, walking home from my aunt's house on a path rarely used that time of the evening. How would you handle it if it were your best friend?"

"Honestly, I'd be curled up in a ball on the floor crying my eyes out, but different people react to tragedy in different ways. Maybe it hasn't fully sunk in yet what's happened."

"Or maybe she's fully expecting the next attempt on her life to succeed," I said. There had been something about my aunt's behavior all day that I hadn't been able to lay a finger on until that very moment. She'd resigned herself to being the next victim. After accepting the fact that her days, even her hours, were probably numbered, it was no wonder she was going about her business as though nothing had happened. How else could she cope with it?

"Pat, are you still there?"

"I'm here," I said, coming out of my fog. "You've just given me something to think about, that's all."

"Is that a good thing?"

"Always," I said.

"You and Annie are being careful, aren't you?"

"Mostly," I said.

"Why don't I like the sound of that?" Jenna asked me.

"Well, I didn't feel right about lying to you. Was that the wrong choice?"

Jenna paused quite a bit then herself before she spoke again. "No, your instincts are right on the money. Pat, I've been lied to before by men I cared about, and I always hated it. The plain, unvarnished truth is better in my mind than the prettiest lie, no matter how much it might hurt hearing it."

"Then we're a good match, because I'm terrible at lying. Not enough practice, I guess."

"Let's keep it that way, shall we? Any idea when you're coming home?"

"You don't miss me by any chance, do you?"

"Only every day," she said with a laugh.

"We just got here yesterday," I answered, feeling the joy in my heart explode. Unlike my relationship in the past with Molly, which always seemed to be full of effort, my interactions with Jenna almost always left me smiling.

"I can't help myself," she said, and I could hear the smile in her voice.

"What can I say? I guess I'm just loveable."

"I can think of one thing you could say," she replied.

We weren't at the "I love you" stage yet, but I knew without having to think about it what she needed to hear, which was fortunately something that I was happy enough to tell her. "I miss you, too, Jenna. My days aren't nearly good enough without you in them."

"That's a good boy," she said in a way she might praise a dog for doing the right thing. I found it charming rather than insulting, knowing how much Jenna loved all animals. "I knew you could do it."

"I appreciate your patience," I said.

I was about to ask her if we could get together when Annie and I got back home when she said, "Oops. Here comes Mr. Daniels. I've got to go. Stay safe until you can come back to me."

It was one of the sweetest ways of saying good-bye that I could imagine, and I felt myself smiling as I answered, "I'll do my best." I hesitated, wanting to add something that made her feel as special as she'd just made me feel, but before I could come up with something, I realized that the line was dead. Oh, well. She knew how I felt about her, and that should be enough to hold her until I could tell her in person.

Annie spoke, and until that moment, I hadn't even realized that she'd come back. "Wow, that must have been some phone call. I can't remember the last time I saw that big a smile from you."

"Have you spoken with Timothy today?" I asked her.

"No, but I know that he's so wrapped up in his logs going up that I might as well be here if I can't be with him. The man's obsessed with that cabin he's building."

"Let me think," I said as I scratched my chin. "Who does that sound like? Don't tell me. Give me a second, I'll get it."

"I freely admit it," Annie said. "I love my cabin in the woods." My twin sister leaned forward over the pot and took in a deep breath. "We're cooking now."

"I certainly hope so," I said. "Should we pull the picnic table over closer to the fire? I'm not sure how we're going to seat everyone if they all show up."

"That's right, you didn't hear the latest development," Annie said.

I braced myself for more bad news. "What happened?"

"Nothing dire, so there are no worries on that account. Aunt Della unilaterally decided that we'd be dining inside this evening."

"Is that all?"

"That's it."

Annie looked at me as though she was expecting some pushback, but I just nodded. "That makes sense to me. The temperature is starting to drop, and there aren't enough seats out here anyway, let alone room to put the food that we're going to be serving. It's not a bad idea."

"Wow, you really are warming up to her, aren't you?"

"I'm trying. After all, when it comes down to it, I'm just as mature as the next guy," I answered.

"That's what I'm afraid of," Annie replied, showing a grin to take the sting out of her comment, not that I thought she'd been taking a shot at me. After all, I agreed with her. Grown men could act like boys with the slightest provocation, and not everyone found that behavior charming.

I poked the coals again and saw that they were beginning to break apart, losing their ability to throw off the heat we needed. "Should I start another batch of charcoal?"

"That's probably not a bad idea," she said, and I pulled twenty more briquettes out of the bag. At home I would have used my briquette chimney, a neat sheet metal contraption that allowed the coals to light and burn at the optimal rate, but here I just stacked them in a pyramid and lit them as best I could. Soon enough they were afire, and ten minutes later, they were ready to put in place of the spent ones that had now devolved into white ash.

"In half an hour, we'll need ten more," she said.

"To brown the top of the ribs, right?" I asked.

"Hey, you're pretty good at this, too, aren't you?"

"What can I say? I'm related to someone who's an expert in outdoor Dutch oven cooking. Some of it was bound to rub off on me sooner or later."

"That's always been my hope and dream," Annie said with a faint smile. "Why don't you throw another log onto the fire? I'd like to keep it going until we're ready to go in."

I did as she suggested, ready for any excuse to add to the flames. I was glad that I'd pushed the pile of burning logs to one side, so we'd still have that heat to warm up to. The briquettes were nice, and they were certainly dependable, but there was something about a real fire with hard wood outside that I loved; whether it was the radiant heat, the leaping flames, the delightful smells, or the wood smoke leaping up to the sky, I couldn't say. All in all, it was a nice place to be, despite a murder having occurred so close by, and so recently at that, and I could see why our aunt loved her home and why the mayor had moved next door, in spite of, or because of, his feelings for Della.

———— ❧ ————

I was about to ask Annie something else about our list of suspects when I heard someone calling out to us down along the lake path.

It appeared that our chance to discuss what happened next was over.

We had company, and based on who it was, I knew that we needed to watch what we said from there on out.

———— ❧ ————

"I see you found the firewood," Davis Morton said as he approached. As he warmed his hands over the fire, he looked at the Dutch oven and the charcoal briquettes on it. "You know, when you told me you were using charcoal, I thought you were crazy. I don't know why, but I just figured that you'd be cooking with the wood, too."

"We can do that, and often at home we do just that," Annie explained, "but this way we'll get a consistent heat throughout the process. Not that we aren't enjoying your wood, too. It makes a great fire."

"I'm happy to have someone burn some of it," he said. "I haven't had a fire in weeks, myself."

Was he sharing a little trivial information with us, or was he trying to alibi himself if we'd found the murder weapon? I couldn't possibly know yet, but I wanted to find out. "Don't you like having a fire?" I asked him.

"Sure, outside it's fun, but I hate the smell of wood smoke in the house. I had a fire at Christmas, but the hearth has been stone cold ever since, and come to think of it, I haven't had one outside, either." He glanced down at the flames. "It seems to be doing a pretty good job of it, isn't it?"

"Grade A," I said. "It must be tough living in that big old house by yourself."

"No more than it is for your aunt to be alone in her quaint little cottage," the mayor said. "Besides, I manage to keep myself busy."

"I'll bet you do," I said. "It's a shame someone had to ruin this tranquil place with murder."

"What are you going to do? The world's gotten to be a dangerous place," he said calmly.

"Have the police managed to dig up any more leads?" Annie asked him.

"About that. I've been meaning to discuss that with you. I shouldn't have said anything about what they found down the path. I got ahead of myself."

"We didn't say a word to anyone, if that's what you're worried about," I said.

"I'm sure that you haven't," he replied, though he really had no reason to believe that, "but Chief Cameron is playing this one pretty tight to the vest, and he's warned me not to talk to you about it anymore."

"You're the mayor, Davis," Annie said. "Can he do that?"

"I may be his boss on paper, but he runs the show when it comes to law enforcement here, and besides, he's not entirely wrong. We need to work together, not against each other. Anyway, I just thought I owed you an explanation as to why I wouldn't be sharing any more information with you about the case."

"But he still believes that the flashlight was the weapon that precipitated her drowning, right?" I asked him.

"Pat, I just told you I couldn't talk about that."

"This isn't new; it's about something you already told us," I countered. "Was the flashlight used to knock her out or not?"

"I hate myself for having to say this, but you aren't giving me in any choice," Davis said. "No comment."

"That's a first," I said with a wry smile. "You must be the only newspaperman to ever give that response to a question from someone who's not writing a story."

"Don't kid yourself. It happens all of the time. You'd be amazed at how many civilians meddle in police investigations."

"Was that a direct shot at us?" I asked him coolly. The mayor's tune had changed quite a bit since the day before, and I wondered what kind of leverage Chief Cameron was using on him.

"It applies wherever it applies," he said. "Let's talk about more pleasant things, shall we? What smells so good?"

"We're having rubbed pork baby back ribs, caramelized onions, green peppers, and carrots."

"Wow, my mouth is watering already. When do we eat?"

"It will be at least half an hour," she said. "Pat, go ahead and add the last batch of briquettes to the top."

I did as she suggested, and then it was just a matter of waiting for the meat to brown up. Patience wasn't necessarily my strong suit, but Annie had acquired a great deal of it, at least when it came to cast iron cooking. The best results were generated from low and slow cooking, and she'd learned from experience not to try to rush the process.

"I'm going in and talking to Della," he said. "I'll see you two later."

After he was out of earshot, I asked, "Should one of us go in with him?"

"You can go. I'm watching the ribs," Annie said.

"Fine," I replied as I put down the last piece of wood I'd been ready to add to the fire. "I may not be as diplomatic as you are, but I'll give it a shot."

"On second thought, I'll go," Annie answered. "Rotate the lid every seven minutes so we get an even browning."

"I can do that," I said, happy that I didn't have to go back into the kitchen with Della and Davis. I was usually a pretty levelheaded fellow, at least in my own estimation, but I was off my game, and Annie knew it. I was going to have to give up the resentment I felt toward Della for abandoning my mother all those years ago once and for all, apparently like Annie and Kathleen had already managed to do. After all, I'd done some pretty stupid things in my past. How would I feel if folks continued to hold it against me so many years later? Though the betrayal still felt fresh to me, it had happened a long time ago, and Della was clearly remorseful for her past behavior. It was time to grow up a little and let it go, and the best way I could start to do that was to drop this ridiculous insistence that I not call her my aunt. She was family, and I was doing a disservice to my mother by continuing to hold a grudge against her.

Sometimes it amazed me that no matter how grown up I felt most of the time, there were times when I could still act like a petulant little kid.

CHAPTER 16: ANNIE

I WAS GLAD THAT I'D VOLUNTEERED to take Pat's place inside. I knew that my brother was perfectly capable of watching our meal, but I still wasn't so sure that he would have been all right in the house with Aunt Della and Davis. He'd come around soon enough; I knew that without the slightest doubt. My brother was a fine and good man, someone who made me proud to be so closely related to.

"Della, they need to go," Davis said as I started into the kitchen where the two of them were having a whispered conversation. Neither of them had seen me, so I quickly ducked back into the corridor.

"Davis, they're my family. I can't just ask them to leave, especially after I abandoned them and their mother all those years ago. It wouldn't be right, and I'm not going to do it."

"They're stirring up trouble here for you," the mayor said. "Do you want all of your neighbors and friends turning on you?"

"I don't see how Annie and Pat are causing that," Della said.

"I've already had several complaints about them," the mayor said. "Cam's on my back to make them disappear, and I can't say I blame him this time. How's he supposed to investigate Cheryl's murder if they keep mucking around in his business?"

That was interesting. I would love to know which citizens of Gateway Lake in particular had complained about us. Maybe if I stayed quiet long enough, I'd find out.

"Need I remind you that I asked them to come here? Someone's been trying to kill me, and I believe that without the twins' presence here, I'd already be dead."

Pat suspected that as well, and I had no reason to dispute it. It was nice seeing our aunt sticking up for us, given the vehemence of the mayor's pleas.

"Are we really going to go over this again? I told you before they even showed up that the snowman falling from the roof and the parade push were both just accidents. Who was there to catch you when you nearly fell? I was standing right there, and I didn't see a soul try to push you in front of that fire truck."

"What about the poison at the supper?" she asked him.

"Della, you got some bad food," he said. "It could have happened to any of us."

"But it didn't, did it? It happened to me. You're not forgetting Cheryl Simmons, are you? She was murdered in my jacket coming from my house at night. How could that possibly be a coincidence?"

"Cheryl had enemies of her own," Davis said.

"None that I know of," Della said, the shock and surprise clear in her voice. "Who could possibly want to hurt her?"

"I'm not at liberty to discuss that, but rest assured, the police chief has his suspects," Davis said. "You're going to have to take my word for it. If you'd let Chief Cameron handle the situation, nobody will bother you again."

"I didn't realize that the two of you had gotten so close all of a sudden, Davis," she told him.

"We haven't always seen eye to eye, it's true, but I have big plans for this small town, and Cam is finally on board now. He wants to see this area grow just as much as I do, and if we work together, we'll make it happen. What we don't need, neither one of us, is a black spot on Gateway Lake's image right now. As soon as Cheryl's murder is solved, the police chief and I are going to get busy with our plans, and we won't forget who helped us, either. This could be good for you as well, Della."

I could feel her wavering as she said, "Honestly, Davis, I don't know what to do. When I speak with the twins, I think one thing, but when I talk to you, I start to have my doubts that this isn't all just in my mind."

It was time to step in before Aunt Della decided to send us away. I had a feeling in my gut that if Pat and I left town without finding the person who was trying to kill her, we'd never see her alive again. "Hey, there," I said, doing my best to sound happy about interrupting them.

"How long have you been standing there?" Davis asked me, trying to be nonchalant as he asked the question.

"I just came in. Why, what did I miss?" I looked at him impishly, hoping to get some kind of rise out of him, but he was too good a politician to let anything slip.

"We were just talking about how excited we were to taste those ribs of yours," he said. "Isn't that right, Della?"

This was the moment of truth. Depending on what my aunt said next, I'd know whose side she was really on. "Actually, the mayor was just urging me to send you and your brother away," she said, her face flushing as she did so.

"Honestly, it wasn't anything as dramatic as all of that," Davis said, backpedalling quickly. "I just mentioned that the police chief is having trouble getting folks to discuss the case with him after you two got them all stirred up."

"Who exactly did we stir up?" I asked sweetly.

"They were his words, not mine," Davis was quick to add. "If you want anything more specific than that, you'll have to talk to him about it."

"Oh, believe me, we will," I said. I took my aunt's hands in mine as I said, "There's something you should know. We're not leaving until we get to the bottom of this, and that's a promise. Nobody else in town might believe you, but Pat and I do."

"That's all I need to know," she said.

"Well, if you'll excuse me, I just remembered some work I have to do back at the office that's rather pressing," the mayor said.

"Does that mean you won't be coming back for dinner?" I asked him with a smile. Maybe I was gloating about my victory a little, but who cared?

"I can't make any promises, but I'll do my best to make it," he said, and then he beat a hasty retreat.

After he was gone, I said, "Thanks for having our backs, Aunt Della."

"That's what family's all about," she said. "It took me a long time to realize that, but it's etched in my heart now. I just wish I could ask your mother for her forgiveness."

"Mom would have given it freely, and you know it, but allow me to do it by proxy. On behalf of the Marsh clan, we all forgive you."

Were there tears in her eyes? I couldn't tell as she asked, "Even Pat?"

"He's coming around," I assured her.

"I can't tell you how happy I am to hear that. Maybe with Davis bowing out, we'll have enough food, at any rate."

"Do you think he's not really coming back?" I asked her.

"Who knows? I've long given up any hope of figuring out what goes on in a man's mind."

I laughed, and then I said, "If it's any consolation, Pat feels the same way about us. Now, what can I do to help you in here?"

"Shouldn't you be out tending your food?" she asked.

"Pat's more than capable of handling things out there," I replied. "Besides, I wanted to spend a little time alone with you."

"That would be delightful," she said. "Grab some plates and cutlery and set the big table, if you don't mind."

"That's why I'm here," I said. As I did as I was told, I thought about the mayor's urgent pleadings that we leave town. Had that really come from the police chief, or did the mayor want us gone for his own reasons? Either way, it wasn't going to happen. I'd close the Iron's grill for good if I had to, but I'd meant what I'd said.

Pat could go back if he wanted to, but I was staying put until this mess was over, one way or the other.

"Yoo-hoo. Is anyone home?" a woman's voice called out from the front parlor. "Your front door was unlocked, so I let myself in."

"No worries, Henrietta," Della said, rolling her eyes a little so I could see it, but not her friend. "We're back here."

The older woman came in carrying a casserole dish covered in foil. "I brought my famous green bean surprise," she said.

"Wonderful," Della said. "Should we reheat it for you now?"

"Just put it in the warming oven, and it will be fine. I find that it's better once it's cooled and been reheated," she said. "Della, may I use the powder room? I meant to go before I left the house, but then I forgot all about it."

"You know where it is," my aunt told her. After Henrietta was gone, Della said, "I don't know why she keeps making this dish. The only surprise about it is that no one eats it, and yet she insists on showing up with it at the slightest provocation. The woman must buy green beans in fifty-gallon drums."

"Is it really that bad?" I asked with a conspiratorial smile. It was nice to have another woman in the family to share inside jokes with besides my older sister.

"Try some for yourself, but don't take more than a spoonful if you value your life," Della said.

"Maybe that's what really poisoned you at the dinner," I said, realizing immediately that I'd gone too far. "I'm sorry. I didn't mean that."

"It's fine," Della said, but evidently the impact of what I'd just said went beyond offending my aunt.

"You were poisoned?" Henrietta asked from the doorway. "What happened, and why didn't you tell me about it?"

I shot a look of apology at my aunt as she explained, "It wasn't anything quite so dramatic. I must have gotten something a little off at the town supper that didn't agree with me."

"I thought you looked a little green around the gills," Henrietta said. "That's why I don't like to eat anything that I don't prepare myself." She frowned for a moment before adding, "Not that I'm sure your food won't be delightful."

"I won't be offended if you eat just your casserole," I said, doing my best not to smile.

"If I did that, then I'd be depriving the others," Henrietta said with a perfectly straight face. "I'll make you a deal. You try my specialty, and I'll try yours."

"It's a deal," I said, trying not to show my reluctance at making the promise. "Now, if you two will excuse me, I'd better go check on Pat."

Della just shook her head and smiled as I walked out the door.

<hr/>

"What happened in there?" Pat asked as he finished turning the lid on the Dutch oven a quarter turn. "I didn't think you were ever coming back."

"I thought you had this all handled," I said, fighting the temptation to lift the lid and check on the progress of the ribs and veggies. Steam was an important part of the cooking process, which was why I'd added water in the first place, though broth, beer, or wine would have done nicely as well. Every time I lifted the lid, I slowed that progression, so it was important to let it go and trust the process.

"I do," he said. "But I still want to know what took you so long."

"Well, before I could walk in and announce myself, I heard the mayor trying to coax our aunt into throwing us out as soon as possible."

"You're kidding," Pat said, and then he studied my expression for a moment. "You're not kidding, are you?"

"No, sir. Evidently the police chief is putting pressure on him to make it happen."

"So, it's Chief Cameron who wants us gone, not the mayor."

"If we can believe Davis," I said. "What if he's the one who wants us to leave town, but he's using the police chief as an excuse? If what he said was true, the two of them are thick as thieves. Apparently they have big plans for this place, and now they're working together."

"That's interesting," Pat said. "Ultimately, that might mean that the police chief is innocent."

"How's that?"

"If he's got big plans with the mayor, why would he plant evidence there that makes the man look guilty of murder?"

"Do we think that branch was planted there now?" I asked him.

"I've had some time to think about it, Annie. What I'm beginning to realize is that the killer could have thrown that stick anywhere, or even drop it on the ground right where he hit Cheryl with it. The only thing gained by stashing it under the deck is to frame the mayor for murder. I have a feeling that there's going to be an anonymous phone call to the police tipping them off about the weapon any minute."

"Let them search all they want to," I said. "We both know where that branch is. Going on that reasoning, it actually narrows our field of suspects more than that."

"How so?"

"Do you honestly think that Serena would set up the man she's clearly in love with, no matter how much she denies it? If we'd found that branch here near Della's backyard, it would make sense that she could have done it, but finding it under Davis's deck means that whoever did it isn't afraid to set him up for a fall, and that eliminates Serena."

"It makes sense when you look at it that way," he said. "If we're right, then that takes Davis off our list, and Cameron and Serena, too. I like it."

"I do, too. We might be wrong about it, but our reasoning makes sense to me. So, where does that leave us?"

"We still have Gary White's name on our list, by the process of elimination. Funny thing is, he's the only one *not* coming to our little dinner this evening," Pat said with a smile.

"Our basic premise is still a mighty big stretch," I told him. "We have to keep our eyes on the rest of them just in case, but I think we should focus on Gary for the time being. I never even considered the possibility that Davis was being set up. You have a devious mind, little brother."

"What can I say? It comes from hanging out with bad company," Pat said with a grin. "If we're right, then we can go after Gary, but if we're wrong, we still need to watch the rest of them like hawks. Where is the mayor, by the way? Is he still inside with Della? I'm still not completely convinced that it's safe to leave her alone with him."

I was touched by my brother's concern for our aunt's well-being. "No, he left fifteen minutes ago. Did you not see him come by?"

"No one's been through here since you went inside," Pat said.

"He must have gone around the front. Anyway, Aunt Della isn't alone. Henrietta Long is in there with her." I told him about making an ill-timed joke about being poisoned, since Henrietta had brought some rather suspect food with her. "It serves me right. Now I have to taste it."

Pat grinned. "I'll try some, too."

"You don't have to."

"I know, but I'm not going to let you experience that without going through it myself. After all, we have each other's backs, no matter what."

"Maybe you'd better let me eat my bite first," I said. "I might need you to drive me to the emergency room."

"Can it really be all that bad?" my brother asked me.

"According to Aunt Della, it's worse. Isn't it about time to rotate that again?" I asked as I pointed to the lid.

"I have another two and a half minutes left," Pat said.

"That's oddly precise."

"Not really. I set the alarm on my cellphone," he said. "Now it's two minutes and eleven seconds. Ten, nine, eight, seven."

I interrupted him before he could get to six. "I don't need a second-by-second update; I know how to count down to zero."

"I don't doubt it for one second," Pat said, and smiled gently at me. A moment later he looked over my shoulder and waved. "It appears our next guest is arriving for the festivities, Annie."

I looked back to where he'd just waved and saw Serena Jefferson approaching.

"Where's Davis? Is he inside?" she asked us breathlessly as she joined us.

"He was, but then he had to leave at the last second," I said.

Her disappointment couldn't have been more evident. "Did he say where he was going?"

"No, just that he forgot to do something back at the office," I said.

"I'll bet he didn't sign the extension for the water permit with the county," she said. "I'd better go help him find it."

"He seemed perfectly capable of handling it himself," I said, but it was in vain.

Serena was already gone.

"Man, she really does have it bad for that man, no matter how hard she protests the fact," I said.

"Which means that we're right. If it's true, it means that she'd never set him up," Pat replied.

"Unless she's playing us all," I answered as the police chief came up the path, this time carrying a bottle of wine in one hand.

As Chief Cameron tried to hand it to me, he said, "I don't know if this is any good or not. It was ten bucks, so there you go."

I glanced at the label and saw that it was a decent wine. "You should take that inside."

"Is Della alone in there?" he asked.

"No, Henrietta's in there."

"Then I'd better go save her. Once that woman starts talking, she never shuts up." As he walked past, he lingered for a moment at the Dutch oven. "Smells good."

"I'm glad you approve," I said.

He didn't get the irony as he headed for the house. Or maybe he did. He paused and then turned back to us. "Listen, I want to apologize to you."

"For what?" Pat asked.

"I've been tough on you, but it's been more out of frustration than anything else. I happened to like Cheryl Simmons, and someone killing her right under my nose is driving me crazy. Anyway, I didn't mean anything personal with anything I might have said or done. Okay?"

"Okay," I said but then added quickly, "Are you taking the threats against my aunt's life seriously?"

"I take everything that happens in my town seriously," he said, and then he made his way up to the house.

"Fancy that," I said after he was gone.

"I wouldn't have believed it if I hadn't been standing right here myself," Pat answered. "We're going to have a crowd, aren't we?"

"That's what I was originally hoping for, but now I'm not so sure," I said. "In case we're wrong about Gary White, I need you to be an extra set of eyes for me tonight."

"Happy to do it," Pat said. "What exactly am I watching for?"

"Anything that looks suspicious to you. If we're wrong about Gary, then we might have the killer amongst us, so we still have to be vigilant."

"That could be a tall order, given how many people are going to be inside," Pat answered.

"I have faith in you."

Pat's phone alarm suddenly went off, and he turned the lid another quarter turn. "That should do it, shouldn't it?"

I took a chance and peeked under the lid. "It looks good to me now."

"Just the same, let's give it seven more minutes," he said.

"What's wrong? Are you concerned about going inside?"

"Actually, I am."

His confession surprised me. "Pat, are you afraid of one of our dinner guests?"

"As a matter of fact, you've got me jumpy about the green bean casserole," he answered with a grin.

CHAPTER 17: PAT

W E ENDED UP HAVING A crowd after all, even though my twin sister and I were beginning to have serious doubts that any of them could be the killer. As Annie and I brought in the main course, I was surprised to see that Davis and Serena had made it back in time to eat after all. There wasn't going to be enough food based on what Annie had prepared in the Dutch oven, but Della— Aunt Della, I corrected myself—had brought out some of the food she'd served us at lunch, and it looked like it was going to be a real feast.

Before we could all dig in, Annie nudged me to get my attention, and then she said, "Before we eat, I'd like to raise a glass to Cheryl Simmons. I didn't have the privilege of knowing her, but I'm sure that she will be missed by one and all."

As Annie spoke, I looked around the room. Davis and the police chief both frowned at the mention of the murder victim's name, Serena didn't have the slightest expression at all, while Della and Henrietta both started tearing up. Neither of the older women's reactions surprised me. After all, they'd both just lost a friend. Had the men's frowns been brought on by memories of the woman's death, or were they upset that Annie and I wouldn't leave it alone? I couldn't tell, but the night was still young.

"Now, let's eat," Della said after a moment's silence.

"Pat, may I speak with you for a minute?" Annie asked me.

"Of course," I said as I followed her into the front parlor, a place deserted, at least for the moment.

"Well? Did you see anything?" she asked me.

I recounted my observations, and she nodded in agreement. "That matches what I noticed as well. Any idea of what any of it might mean?"

"Not a clue," I confessed. "We need to keep digging, just in case our theory about the hardware store owner is wrong."

"Maybe I should have pushed them all a little harder when I toasted Cheryl's memory," Annie said.

"If you'd done that, Aunt Della and Henrietta would have both started bawling."

"Hey, you just called...never mind." Annie adjusted quickly.

"I'm trying," I said, knowing what she'd been about to say.

"Good for you," Annie said. "What should we do now?"

"There's only one thing we can do. We need to keep pushing."

"That sounds like a plan to me."

I was about to rejoin the crowd with Annie when my phone rang. Was Jenna calling me back already? No, it was Kathleen instead.

"Go on," I told Annie as I answered the call.

She nodded, and I said, "Hey, stranger. How's it going?"

"That's why I'm calling you. Have you been making any progress on the case?"

I brought her up to date on both of our latest theories, one that the hardware store owner was behind all of the mayhem and the other that the rest of our suspects were gathered at Aunt Della's place for dinner. "Do you have thoughts that might help us?" I asked her as I finished.

"No, it sounds as though you're doing all that you can. I wish I could be there with you."

"Sure, then you'd get to share the bed with Annie, but I'd still be stuck out on the couch."

"I'm serious, Pat."

"So am I. Listen, we're doing all that we can. If we haven't made any progress by tomorrow night, I'll call you back."

"You'd better. Be careful, little brother."

"I resent the fact that everybody treats me like I'm the baby in the family, even though it's only by seven minutes in Annie's case."

"Talk to her. You're both my younger siblings."

After I hung up, I saw that Annie was lingering nearby. "Who was that?"

"Kathleen was checking up on us," I said.

"Did she have any good ideas for us?"

"No, she thought we were doing a good job."

"That's a good thing, right?" Annie asked.

"I suppose, but we're still not much further than we were when we first got here."

"Cheer up. At least we get to go eat now," Annie said with a smile.

———————

We didn't get our food immediately, though. We got distracted by what we found in the dining room, though it was no real surprise when we found Serena hanging on every word Davis was saying. We joined the group as the mayor held forth on what a success the Winter Wonderland festival had been, praising the two women who had been the driving forces behind it. "Folks came from all over to see our town at its best. Della, you and Henrietta did marvelous work."

Aunt Della smiled, but all Henrietta would do was blush from the attention. Our aunt said, "Not only was it good PR for Gateway Lake, but we should make a profit from it as well."

"Let's not be too hasty saying that," Henrietta said cautiously. "After all, we still need to go over the books and write the last few checks before we can say how we did one way or the other."

"When are you going to have a final accounting to present us?" the mayor asked them.

"Tomorrow noon at the latest," Della promised.

"I'm not sure we can have everything ready by then," Henrietta said with some reluctance. "You should see my desk at home. It's covered with invoices, receipts, and all kinds of paperwork."

Aunt Della patted her friend's shoulder. "I didn't mean to leave the burden of dealing with most of the finances to you. I'll be over first thing tomorrow morning, and we won't rest until we've got it all sorted out. How's that sound?"

"I'd appreciate all of the help I can get. Are you making any progress on Cheryl's murder?" Henrietta asked the police chief. "The entire town is buzzing about it."

"We're following up on some leads," Cameron said.

"That's cop talk for you don't really have a clue, isn't it?" I said.

"Pat, I wasn't speaking in code. We've got a few theories we're actively pursuing right now. That's what professionals do, you know. We investigate, interview, and evaluate the evidence."

"It sounds as though anyone could do that," Annie said, backing me up.

"Not without our resources," he said.

"Let's talk about something less depressing, shall we?" Serena asked. "How long are we going to have those snowmen looming all over town? I saw one the other day that I could swear was staring straight at me."

"I don't know. I kind of like having them around," the mayor said.

"Of course, they do have a certain charm," Serena added, quickly backpedaling from her former position.

"That's because you've never had one try to kill you," Aunt Della said.

"Do you really think that was an attempt on your life?" Davis asked her.

"All I'm saying is that it's odd that it happened precisely when I was standing under it."

"I don't know," Cam said. "It all sounds a little too farfetched to me."

"So you've said," Aunt Della said.

We weren't getting anywhere, though Annie and I kept trying to draw out our guests about the murder and the other attempts on Della's life. Finally, Annie pulled me aside again.

"Pat, the more we speak with these people, the more I believe that none of them had anything to do with the attempts on Aunt Della's life. It's Gary White. I just know it."

"What should we do about it?"

"I know you're not going to like this, but we need to tell Chief Cameron our theory, and more importantly, we need to give him that tree branch."

I looked hard at my sister before I spoke. "Are you sure that's the next step we should take?"

"It's making me paranoid just having that thing in the back of my car. The sooner we can hand it over to the authorities, the better, as far as I'm concerned."

I realized that Annie was probably right. There were things we could do just as well as local law enforcement, but this was in the police department's area of expertise, not ours. "You're right. Let's do it."

I walked back into the dining room where everyone was still chatting and cornered the chief. "Do you have a second?"

"Why?" he asked skeptically. I clearly was not one of his favorite people at the moment, despite his earlier apology, but perhaps that was about to change when I told him what I'd found.

"It's important."

That quieted the crowd.

"Fine," Chief Cameron said reluctantly. "What's up?"

"Let's find Annie first," I said.

"We'll all be right here when you're finished," Aunt Della said, and then she turned to Henrietta. "Did you do something different with that famous casserole of yours?"

"I added bacon bits," she said proudly. "Did you like it?"

"I could really tell a difference," my aunt said, neatly sidestepping the question. I'd tasted it, and Della had been right. The stuff had been dreadful, with or without the added bacon bits.

Annie was waiting for us by the door, and as Chief Cameron approached, he said, "Okay, you two. Make it quick."

"We found the real murder weapon. It wasn't the flashlight," I said without preamble.

"What are you talking about?" he asked. I had his attention now.

"While I was gathering some firewood under Davis's deck, I

stumbled across a sawn-off tree branch with hair and fiber still clinging to the bark. Somebody's trying to set the mayor up to make it look as though he's the killer, but we have a hunch who really did it."

"Where is it right now?" he asked. "I'm warning you, if you're playing games with physical evidence, I'm locking you both up on the spot."

"The only reason we moved it is because we were afraid someone might try to use it against him," I said. "It's out in Annie's trunk."

"Actually, it's more of a cargo area," she corrected me.

"I don't care if it's a kangaroo pouch, let's see it."

I called out, "We'll be right back, Aunt Della."

Annie looked at me with approval as Della answered, "Take your time, dears."

Once we were outside, I told the chief, "We think you should be looking at Gary White for the murder."

"Why would you think that?"

"He had a fight with Della and threatened her. Besides, he's the only one of our suspects who could possibly want to frame the mayor for it." I explained our rationale proudly.

The pride didn't last very long. "I hate to burst your bubble, but Gary's got a rock-solid alibi for the time of the murder."

"What?! That's impossible!" Annie and I had been so sure of it.

"How could you know? He was canoodling with one of his employees all night, and she's signed a statement that he never left her sight covering the entire time we know that Cheryl was murdered."

"And you believe her?" Annie asked.

"I do. She's my cousin, and she doesn't lie. Tillie might not use the best judgment when it comes to her personal life, but I've never known the girl to lie to me. As far as I'm concerned, you can take it to the bank."

"So, where does that leave us?" I asked.

"I don't know about the two of you, but it leaves me exactly where I was before. Like I said before, we're making progress, and we'll continue to work toward finding the killer until we're satisfied that we've got the right person."

Annie popped open her trunk, and for a moment, I was afraid that someone had broken in and stolen the branch in question, but to my relief, it was exactly where we'd left it. The police chief leaned over and picked up the branch, being careful to use the edge of a small plastic bag to grab it. As he held it aloft, I noticed a glint of light coming from the house, and when I turned, I saw every last one of our dinner guests watching us closely. Why was I not surprised? "What should we tell them when we go back in?" I asked the police chief.

"Tell them whatever you want to," he said. "I'm taking this straight to my office and having my people check it out."

"You're just going to leave us here?" Annie asked.

The police chief's only response was just to smile at us as he walked away, so my sister and I had no choice.

We turned and walked back inside.

<hr>

It didn't take long for the party to break up, especially when Annie and I feigned ignorance about why the chief had left so abruptly. No one was willing to push us any further, but it seemed as though we'd suddenly all run out of things to talk about.

After our guests were all gone, something suddenly occurred to me as we were helping our aunt clean up the kitchen. "I never got any ribs!"

"Don't worry. I'll make some for you when we get back home," Annie said soothingly.

"Just for me?"

"You can share them if you want to," my sister said with a smile.

"And if I don't want to?"

"Then they are all yours."

"I hope that won't be anytime soon," Aunt Della said.

Annie had told me about her plans to stay longer if needed, and I'd agreed. "Not if we haven't made any more headway than we already have. You might have a hard time getting rid of us."

"We'll never know, because I'll never try," she said. We finished the dishes, and Annie stifled a yawn.

"I'm exhausted," she said. "Is anyone else tired?"

"I could go to sleep right here," I admitted. It had been a long and stressful day.

"Then let's all call it a day and get a fresh start tomorrow," Aunt Della suggested, and Annie and I heartily agreed.

All in all, the evening had been a bust, but we couldn't let that discourage us. I took up my place on the couch again and tried to get to sleep, but something kept nagging at the back of my mind. Had I missed something over the past few days, something that held the key to our investigation? Whatever it was, I couldn't put my finger on it. The only thing I could do was try to wipe my mind clean, get some sleep, and come at it from a different direction the next day. Even if the sleep didn't help, at least I'd get some rest.

Unfortunately, a long and uninterrupted sleep was the last thing the night had in store for us.

I woke up an untold time later in a cold sweat, and I could swear that the temperature in the room was ten degrees colder than it had been when I'd first gone to bed. My dreams, more like nightmares, had been haunted by frigid plywood snowmen chasing me along the river path, taunting me with dollar signs that had sharp sticks slashing through them. I knew that it meant something, but I couldn't for the life of me tell what it was.

I looked around and saw a faint light on in the kitchen, so I got up to investigate.

I found Annie standing in front of the refrigerator peering inside.

"Can't sleep either?" I asked her.

She looked startled suddenly seeing me standing there. "Patrick, you scared the fool out of me. Did I wake you up?"

"No, I had a bad dream," I admitted.

"Was it cowboy zombies?" she asked. I'd had that nightmare once, but in my defense, I'd only been eleven years old at the time.

"No."

"Were you falling through space again?"

"No, it wasn't that, either. Would you give me a chance to tell you?"

"Sorry," she said. "What was it about?"

"I'm not sure I want to tell you now, especially if you're going to bring it up again later."

"What if I promise not to? Come on. Spill it. You know you want to tell me," she said as she got a can of soda and put it on the counter.

"It was about those plywood snowmen that are all over town," I admitted.

"I'm with you on that one. Those things look cool in the daylight, but at night they're downright wicked. What possessed them to paint those leering grins on them?"

"I don't know, but that wasn't the worst part. They were chasing me all through town, and I woke up just as they nearly caught me. Annie, it was in the exact spot where Cheryl Simmons was killed."

"How awful," she said. "That must have been terrifying."

"It was bad enough, but they were carrying dollar signs. Instead of the lines through the shapes, though, they were sharpened sticks."

"Sticks? How odd."

"As if snowmen coming to life and harassing me wasn't enough?" I asked as I grabbed a bottle of water for myself. I didn't know how my sister could drink soda before going to sleep, but I knew that I could never do it.

"What do you suppose it means?" she asked me.

"Beats me," I said as I cracked the plastic top open and took a healthy swallow.

"You know what? I might know," Annie said without touching

her own drink. The expression on her face told me that she was on to something.

"You're kidding."

"Hear me out. What if your subconscious mind was trying to tell you something. I've been wrestling with something, too."

"Angry snowmen?" I asked her.

"Of course not, but we're missing something, and it's right under our noses."

"I know the feeling."

"Who could it be, though? Our reasoning about the others is sound. Unless…"

"Unless what?" I asked her when she didn't finish the sentence.

"What if the killer never made it onto our suspect list?"

"Then I'd say we're out of luck."

"Pat, I've got it," she said suddenly. "Who's been hanging around us the entire time, but we haven't suspected them even once?"

Then I got it myself. "Henrietta Long. It's all about the money, isn't it? That's why the snowmen were chasing me with deadly dollar signs. That's brilliant, Annie."

"Don't give me the credit. You're the one who figured it out, at least on a subconscious level," she said. "The only reason Henrietta could possibly be so reluctant to close the books on the Winter Wonderland must be because she's been stealing from the accounts. Once they do a final reckoning, her thefts will be discovered, so she's got to stop that from happening."

"Even if she kills our aunt," I said, "someone's going to eventually figure it out."

"Not if she blames Aunt Della for all of it," Annie said. "In a way, it's perfect, since our aunt won't be around to defend herself. We're not going to let that happen, though, are we? I'm going to call Chief Cameron right now."

Annie never got a chance to make that call, though.

"Put down the phone," a voice from the edge of the other room said as she stepped out of the shadows.

It was Henrietta Long, and she was holding a pistol in her hand.

"That's why I was so cold," I said, dumbfounded that we'd figured it out, but it was still going to be too late. "You snuck in through a cracked window. Did you unlock it during the party?"

She smiled. "Oh, I did it well before that. While you were outside cooking, I opened it even before I announced my presence. Remember, Annie?"

"I remember," my sister said. "You don't have to do this, you know. I'm sure we can work something out."

Henrietta laughed, but there was no joy in it. "I'm afraid that's not possible. I can't afford to make restitution, and besides, even if I still had the money, I can't bargain away what happened to Cheryl."

"Why did you kill her?" I asked, seeing a form creeping down the stairs just behind her. We must have woken Aunt Della up, but did she have any kind of weapon to defend us all with? Just a short piece of closet rod, not much bigger than the branch Henrietta had used on Cheryl, and the killer had a gun in her hands.

"I thought she was Della," Henrietta explained a little petulantly. "She was wearing your aunt's coat, and when I saw her walking down the path, I hid behind a snowman until she passed me by. When she walked past me, I took a swing at her head. She fell from the impact, and I was going to drag her body into the trees, but then it started to roll down toward the water, and I couldn't stop it. I panicked! As I raced back up the path, I thought about chucking the branch in my hand, but then I decided to use it to my advantage. Why not frame the mayor with the crime? That would surely divert suspicion away from me. I was about to call the police this evening to let them know where they could find the weapon I'd used, and then you two had to go and ruin everything. I haven't even been able to go back home, since you told the police chief that I was the killer."

"We thought it was Gary White," Annie confessed without thinking.

I'd been hoping to use the threat of arrest against Henrietta to get her to spare our lives, but I couldn't blame my sister for blurting it out.

That made Henrietta smile. "So, Cam's not coming for me? Then I still might be able to get away with this. All I need to do is get rid of the three of you, and then I can blame it all on Della."

"How are you going to explain three more homicides and pin it on our aunt?" I asked her as Della got closer. Henrietta seemed as though she'd lost her mind completely with her insane plan, but I needed to keep her talking to give Della a chance to act.

"I won't have to. They'll find your bodies in the morning, they'll go down as three more random acts of violence, and I'll act as shocked as everybody else that this could happen in our quiet little town."

"Exactly how many times did you try to kill our aunt?" I asked her.

Henrietta frowned in frustration. "More than I thought I'd need to. First I tried pushing that wretched plywood snowman off the roof onto her, but the wind caught it on the way down and missed her by a mile. Then I trailed her during the parade, fighting through the crowds, acting as though I just wanted a better look at the festivities. When the opportunity came, I shoved her right in front of the fire truck, but Davis was standing nearby, and he pulled her back to safety! I could have screamed in frustration."

"And the poisoned food at the supper?" I asked her. Even though we might all be about to die, it was good to know that Aunt Della hadn't been crazy. Those really had been sincere attempts on her life by a very determined amateur killer.

"I knew Della was allergic to seafood, so I dosed her chicken with some ground-up shrimp. I thought it would kill her, but it just made her throw up, and after that, she was fine! I didn't know that at the time, though, so when she ran to the restroom, I grabbed her plate and tossed it in the garbage before anybody discovered her body. After that, I knew that I had to get rid of her once and for all, so I cracked a window here earlier. Things would have been so much easier if you two would have just stayed where you were, but in a few minutes, my worries will all be over. My plan is perfect this time."

"Maybe not so perfect after all. That gun doesn't have a silencer on it," Annie said. "Davis will hear the gunshots."

"Thanks for reminding me," Henrietta said. "I'll just grab a pillow to shoot through, and then we'll be set."

As Henrietta turned to reach for a nearby pillow, it was time to act.

I couldn't wait for my aunt anymore, so the second Henrietta turned her back, I leapt at her.

Annie was half a second behind me, and I was happy to see Della swing her club in the air as she approached from another angle altogether.

Unfortunately, she missed completely, Annie's dive came up short, and I barely managed to grab Henrietta's leg before I crashed to the floor myself.

Henrietta must have had her finger on the trigger when we'd lashed out at her, because as she fell, a shot rang out, temporarily blinding and deafening us all with the muzzle flash and the explosion.

At least she hadn't had time to use the pillow as a silencer.

I was nearly blinded by the sudden flash of light, but I couldn't let that stop me.

I still had hold of Henrietta's leg, so I did the only thing I could think of.

I bit her with everything I had.

CHAPTER 18: ANNIE

I WASN'T SURE WHAT MY BROTHER did to Henrietta, but she suddenly began to howl in pain. She instinctively tried to fight him off, but he wouldn't let go of his grip.

Henrietta still had the gun in her hand, but she must have been so startled by what he'd done that she'd completely forgotten about it for the moment and was using it as a bludgeon on his back instead of cocking the trigger and shooting him.

We couldn't count on that being the case for long, though.

I scrambled to my feet and grabbed Henrietta's arm while Aunt Della went for her face with her bare hands, clawing and scratching to make some kind of impact on her attack on Pat.

As I was wrestling the gun away from her, another shot rang out.

None of us were hit, at least as far as I could tell, but my aunt was going to need a new back door window.

That was the last bit of fight Henrietta had left in her.

I had the gun in my hands now.

"Everyone stop what you're doing!" I shouted.

Della reluctantly stopped pounding at her former friend's face, evidently trying to drive the woman's nose through the back of her head. It was bleeding profusely, but I couldn't see that until someone flipped on the light, blinding us all again.

It was Chief Cameron, and I was more relieved to see him than I could say.

"Do you want to put that down on the floor, nice and slow?" he asked me softly. It was only then that I noticed that his weapon was pointed straight at my chest.

"She killed Cheryl," I said, fighting the sobs I felt trying to break free from inside of me.

"Okay. That's fine. No worries here. You can tell me all about it, just as soon as you drop your weapon."

"It's not mine. It's hers." Was I babbling? I felt as though I was babbling.

"It's over, Annie. We won. Drop the gun," Pat said calmly, finally getting through to me.

My brother's words finally hit home, and I let the weapon fall from my hands to the floor.

Chief Cameron sighed loudly, and then he holstered his own weapon as he pulled out a pair of handcuffs.

"Did you hear the shots? Is that how you got here so quickly?" I asked him as he approached Henrietta, who appeared to have gone completely comatose.

"I was next door at Davis's place," he said. After studying the murderer for a moment, he asked, "What did you do to her?"

Pat said simply, "I bit her."

"I hit her with an old closet rod," Della said proudly.

"And I grabbed the gun away from her," I finished.

"Wow, you three really did a number on her. I'm going to have to call an ambulance."

"Save your sympathy for someone who deserves it, Chief," Della said. "She came here to kill us."

"Why?" he asked.

"Money," I answered. "She stole from the Winter Wonderland, and she had no other way of covering her tracks but to kill us all."

"Is that true, Henrietta?" Aunt Della asked her.

There was no response. The lights were on, but nobody was home.

⟶⟶◈⟵⟵

After Henrietta was gone and we'd agreed to come to the station to sign statements, it was just the three of us again. I knew that we wouldn't have much time to be alone, though. Since Davis had heard the shots too, once he got the all clear, I knew the mayor would be there, along with most of the rest of the town. Now that Aunt Della had been fully vindicated in her belief that someone had indeed been trying to kill her all along, I had a guess that her stock in town was going to be on the rise.

My aunt was sweeping up broken glass when I tried to take the broom from her. "Are you okay?"

"I'm still in shock, I think," she said as she let the broom slip through her hands. "If it hadn't been for the two of you, I'd be dead right now."

"We all might have been dead if Pat hadn't acted so quickly," I said. "He figured it out, and then he distracted Henrietta long enough to give us a chance. He's the real hero."

"Don't be so modest," my brother replied. "I may have had the dream about the killer snowmen, but you're the one who figured it out first."

"Okay, we're both heroes," I said with a smile. "What made you think to bite her? Not that I'm complaining. It was a stroke of genius."

"I didn't have much leverage on her leg, and I expected to get shot anyway, so I figured why not give her something to remember me by? If you two hadn't sprung to my aid, she would have killed me. There's no doubt in my mind about that."

"So, we're all heroes," I said, "including you, Aunt Della."

"I couldn't just let her shoot you, could I?" she asked.

"Well, we appreciate the fact that you felt that way," I said with a grin. "I've got an idea. When this is all over, why don't you come to Maple Crest and visit me at my cabin? It's not much, and we'll be a little snug, but I'd love for you to see the place. A lot has changed since the last time you were there."

"You don't want to do that, Aunt Della," Pat said. "You know how far out in the woods she lives. You can stay with me. I'll even give you my bed. We already know that I don't mind sleeping on the couch when it's for a good cause."

I looked at my aunt and could see tears tracking down her cheeks.

"I appreciate both your offers, and I do plan to visit soon, but right now, I need to be here, by myself, to get over what happened. If I don't, I'm afraid that I'll never be able to stay, and I do so love this place."

"The invitation is always open," I said.

"The same goes for me," Pat echoed.

"Thank you. Thank you both," she said, and then she wrapped us both up in her arms. "It's so good to have a family again."

"I've got a feeling that you're going to have more than you bargained for," I said. "I called Kathleen while they were hauling Henrietta away, and she's already on the road."

"Then I should put on a pot of coffee," Aunt Della said. "Would you two mind keeping me company?"

"That's why we're here," Pat said, and we all went into the kitchen to wait for the onslaught of visitors we knew that we were about to have, in addition to my older sister.

Henrietta had done something terrible in stealing the money, and then she'd compounded her sins a thousandfold by killing to cover it up. If she ever managed to snap out of her fog, she'd pay for what she'd done, with interest.

As for us, Pat and I had come to Gateway Lake trying to help our estranged aunt, and in the end, we'd brought her fully back into our lives.

As far as I was concerned, that was more valuable than anything Henrietta Long could have ever stolen.

RECIPES

The Iron's Breakfast Frittata

Sometimes a bowl of cereal just isn't enough, especially on holidays and special occasions. When we want to do something out of the ordinary, we make one of these frittatas in a cast iron skillet. The beauty of this dish is that you can add whatever you have handy that sounds good to some basic ingredients, and you have a meal fit for a millionaire—on a common man's budget! We don't normally cook eggs in our cast iron ware, but the material holds the heat beautifully, making this too good a dish to pass up. We have an enamel-coated cast iron skillet just for this meal, though since we first bought it, we use it for other things, too!

Don't be afraid to explore the possibilities!

Ingredients

- 6 large eggs, whisked well
- 1/4 cup milk (whole or 2%)
- 1/4 teaspoon favorite seasoning
- 2 teaspoons butter
- 2 teaspoons olive oil
- Filling (total amount should equal approximately one cup)
- green bell pepper, diced
- sweet onion, diced
- cheese, shredded (we like extra sharp cheddar)
- baby portabella mushrooms, sliced

- cooked ham, diced

Directions

Preheat the oven's broiler.

Beat the eggs in a large mixing bowl, adding the milk and seasoning. Mix well. Add one cup from the fillings listed above (your preference) and stir into the mixture.

On the stovetop, heat your cast iron skillet over medium heat, melting the butter and olive oil. Next, add the egg and filling mixture to the skillet, reduce the temperature to medium low, and cook for 6 to 8 minutes, until the eggs are almost set. Remove from heat, sprinkle the top with shredded cheese, and then place the skillet under the broiler until the eggs are completely set and the top is browned slightly. Remove from the oven and serve while still warm.

Serves 3 to 5 people, depending on the size of the slices.

Cast Iron Crisp Apple Crunch

In our household, no meal is complete without dessert! My late mother-in-law used to serve dessert, usually some type of pie, after every meal, including breakfast. This was clearly a woman after my own heart, and she is dearly missed to this day. I've long been a big fan of Dutch apple pie, so I decided one day to make this variation in my cast iron skillet! We use the enamel-coated skillet mentioned in the recipe above for this treat as well! If you're familiar with my crumb-topping apple pie, then you're in for a bit of déjà vu. This process is the same, with the exception of omitting the bottom crust and baking the ingredients in a cast iron skillet. Though the ingredients are nearly identical, this produces a unique creation.

Give it a try. Not only will you have a tasty treat in the end, but the house will smell amazing all day!

Ingredients

Filling

- 2 Granny Smith apples, sliced
- 1 Pink Lady apple, sliced
- 1/2 cup granulated sugar
- 2 tablespoons white unbleached all-purpose flour
- 1/2 teaspoon ground nutmeg
- 1/2 teaspoon ground cinnamon
- 1 dash of table salt

Topping

- 1 cup all white unbleached all-purpose flour
- 1/2 cup packed brown sugar
- 1/2 cup salted butter, room temperature

Directions

Preheat the oven to 400 degrees F.

Place the sliced apples in a large mixing bowl. In a separate, smaller bowl, mix the sugar, flour, nutmeg, cinnamon, and salt together. Add this dry mixture to the apples and set aside. In another small mixing bowl, add the flour and brown sugar, mixing well. Add the butter and cut in with a fork or a pastry cutter. Heat the skillet over medium heat, add the apple mixture, then the crumb topping. Take off the heat and place your skillet into the oven. Turn every 10 minutes, and when the crumb topping browns nicely, loosely cover with foil and continue baking until a knife pierces an apple slice easily, between 25 and 35 minutes total cooking time, depending on your cast iron, the oven, and the barometric pressure. (Just teasing about that last one, though it might be a factor. Who knows?)

Remove from oven and spoon out healthy portions. Vanilla ice cream added just before consumption takes this to a whole other level.

Serves 3 to 5 people, depending on how big their sweet tooths (or is that sweet teeth?) are.

If you enjoy Jessica Beck Mysteries and you would like to be notified when the next book is being released, please send your email address to newreleases@jessicabeckmysteries.net. Your email address will not be shared, sold, bartered, traded, broadcast, or disclosed in any way. There will be no spam from us, just a friendly reminder when the latest book is being released.

Also, be sure to visit our website at jessicabeckmysteries.net for valuable information about Jessica's books.

OTHER BOOKS BY JESSICA BECK

The Donut Mysteries
Glazed Murder
Fatally Frosted
Sinister Sprinkles
Evil Éclairs
Tragic Toppings
Killer Crullers
Drop Dead Chocolate
Powdered Peril
Illegally Iced
Deadly Donuts
Assault and Batter
Sweet Suspects
Deep Fried Homicide
Custard Crime
Lemon Larceny
Bad Bites
Old Fashioned Crooks
Dangerous Dough
Troubled Treats
Sugar Coated Sins
Criminal Crumbs
Vanilla Vices
Raspberry Revenge

The Classic Diner Mysteries
A Chili Death
A Deadly Beef
A Killer Cake
A Baked Ham

A Bad Egg
A Real Pickle
A Burned Biscuit

The Ghost Cat Cozy Mysteries
Ghost Cat: Midnight Paws
Ghost Cat 2: Bid for Midnight

The Cast Iron Cooking Mysteries
Cast Iron Will
Cast Iron Conviction
Cast Iron Alibi
Cast Iron Motive

32529676R00099

Made in the USA
Middletown, DE
08 June 2016